KILLING
The
SECRET

A Sheriff Lexie Wolfe Novel

Book 1, 2nd Edition

DONNA WELCH JONES

Twisted Plot Publishing

Publisher's Note: *Killing the Secret* is a work of fiction. Names, characters, places, and incidents are products of the author's imagination or are used fictitiously and are not to be construed as real. Any resemblance to actual events, locales, organizations, or persons, living or dead, is entirely coincidental.

Twisted Plot Publishing
© 2017, Donna Welch Jones
Tahlequah, Oklahoma 74464
 Printed in the United States of America

All Rights Reserved.

Except as permitted under the U.S. Copyright Act of 1976, no part of this publication may be reproduced, distributed, or transmitted in any form by any means, or stored in a database or retrieval system, without the prior written permission of the author.

Manufactured in the United States of America

ISBN: 978-0-9970148-5-3 Paperback

Visit the authors' website: www.donnawelchjones.com

Dedication

To My Husband,
Mark H. Jones
In Appreciation For His Love and
Technical Support

Dear Bettie,
I hope you enjoy my book!
Donna Welch Jones

Prologue

He stopped at a roadside café before he killed her, rather than after. Caffeine after 8 p.m. kept him awake. If he overslept, he'd miss his flight. He sure as hell didn't want to spend an extra night in Kansas.

As soon as he walked into the café, he regretted stopping. The fleeting glances from locals made him feel like a flashing light. The nosey bastards reminded him of the people in Diffee. He was glad he'd put on the wig. It camouflaged his identity. Smells of grease, smoke, and sweat from people who obviously didn't believe in daily showers assaulted his senses. It felt as if the odors stuck to his clothes. Nausea roiled in his stomach. He swayed and gripped the edge of the table.

"Are you okay, handsome? I'd take you home with me for some TLC." The blonde waitress made her offer with a crooked smile.

"I want coffee with cream," he ordered, then stared out the window. He must concentrate on why he was in this disgusting place, maybe then his resolve could override the sick feeling. All seven must perish. His second victim, Tina, will die tonight.

Terri, the first, was hardly worth his time. She was dying of cancer, but he knew she must die in his time frame—not God's. Being Catholic might motivate her to confess sins on her deathbed. He wasn't about to give her the chance to ruin his life.

The waitress set the cup down with a bang. Brown droplets splashed on the table, barely missing his linen shirt.

"Sorry, handsome," she cooed.

He suppressed the urge to throw hot coffee in her face. He muttered, "Accidents happen."

She slid her hand softly from his wrist to his elbow.

"Darcy, honey," a man called from the bar. "Can you quit hittin' on the guy long enough to get me a refill?"

The murderer took a swallow, then put a five on the table. He left before the white trash returned.

Chapter One

Sheriff Lexie Wolfe searched for any sign of life in the Oklahoma backwoods from her airplane seat. Smoke was the most likely indication of human life below since it was just above freezing this cold March morning. Tye and Clay, her deputies, sat across from her. Red, the pilot, tore out the four back seats on the old plane and put in benches so he could hire out for parachute jumping. The interior smelled of cheap liquor—a courage booster left from a customer Red had taken out the night before.

The first female sheriff of the small town of Diffee, Lexie had no delusions about why she was elected. Those six years as a cop in Houston and the Masters Degree in Criminology didn't earn the badge on her chest. Sympathy, not experience, won the election. Her brother, Tye, traded his right leg for two lives and a Medal of Honor. Her father was brutally murdered, and she was left for dead when their farmhouse was broken into years ago. Those were her vote getters.

The fine features and blue eyes of her Caucasian mother and the skin coloring of her Cherokee father created a stunning daughter. The illusion of beauty ended up close. Lexie traced the scar down the right side of her face. Her mother raged, cried, and bitched in attempts to force Lexie to have plastic surgery. Storming back, Lexie told her, "My face is a reminder that Dad's killer is somewhere living a life he doesn't deserve. Everyday I touch my scar so my hate won't subside."

"That's sick!" her mother screamed. Lexie's fingers

moved from the scar, and weaved her dark waist-length hair into a single braid. She didn't care why she was elected sheriff. All that mattered was she now had the power and facilities to find the person who murdered her father. Drug busts usually exhilarated her, but today it was a waste of time. She wanted to search records for clues to the murderer instead of jumping out of an airplane.

The hard seat made it impossible for Lexie's butt to find a comfortable position. Her brother, Tye, slept tranquilly across from her even though he had to bend himself to fit.

The Indians won the war of Tye's genes. He showed no physical resemblance to his white mother. His straight black hair was pulled back tightly at the nape of his neck. His skin and eyes were earth shades. Even while sleeping, he exuded strength and a presence.

"I see smoke," Clay pointed downward as he spoke.

"Yep," Red replied. "I better move away from here before someone hears the plane. I'll drop you folks near the clearing about a mile north."

Clay checked his parachute. His blond curly hair and big blue eyes resulted in his nickname 'pretty boy.' Clay didn't require a deputy application to get his job. All he could enter was cute, Mayor's DNA, twenty-three, and spoiled.

Tye removed his prosthesis.

Clay's eyes widened, "Don't you need that leg?"

"Not when I hit the ground. Better to have one leg and hop for a while." Tye laughed as he strapped the false limb to his body. "Don't worry! I'll get ready fast enough to follow you and Lexie."

"I'll wait for you," Clay made a sweeping hand motion. "Age before beauty."

Tye responded with the middle finger of his right hand.

"Ladies first." Tye bowed towards Lexie. "Or should I say sheriff first?"

"Don't harass me, big brother. You know I can fire you."

"Sure, like you'd fire a super hero."

"I'm out of here," Lexie countered, "before the weight of your ego brings this plane down."

"I think I'll wait here," were Clay's last words before Tye pushed him through the opening.

Tye hit the ground then quickly attached his leg. Lexie helped Clay unravel his cord from a small pine that barely missed extinction from the rough landing.

The three of them tracked toward the meth house hidden in the woods. After forty minutes, they found the small frame structure.

"You guys guard the back," Lexie directed. She slowly opened the front door. The ammonia smell engulfed her and watering eyes blurred her vision.

"Wilbur Langley!" she hollered. "Come out!" She heard footsteps moving toward her. She pulled a gun from inside her jacket.

"Mommy! Mommy!" a child cried out. He ran toward her then hugged a leg. His diaper bagged in the back from the weight of urine and feces, exposing his little red butt.

"Come back here, stupid Gabriel," the older child ordered. "She's goin' shoot you."

"I'm not shooting anyone." Lexie pushed the gun into its holster.

"Why you got a gun then?" asked the big brother.

Tye winked at Lexie, "That's a good question."

"I removed it in case someone tried to hurt us," Lexie

explained in a soft voice.

"Well, my daddy would get you if he was here. He hates sheriffs."

Tye put his hand on the child's head. "What's your name, boy?"

"Seth."

"Are your mommy and daddy around, Seth?"

"No, but Mommy said she'd hurry back."

"You're going to town with us," Lexie said.

"We can't leave." Seth's small hands grasp his waist. His chin lifted as he looked at Lexie. His body stiffened—ready to fight.

"Your little brother is hungry," Tye reasoned. "I don't see any food. Are you supposed to take care of him?"

Seth hung his head, "Yep," he murmured.

Lexie took a cue from her brother. "If you stay here he'll get sick, then your mom will get angry. You'll have to change that dirty diaper if you don't come with us."

"Yuck," Seth's face pinched in disgust. "We'll go."

Tye gathered evidence from the kitchen while Clay kept watch outside. Lexie ripped the old tablecloth in half and folded it into a new diaper for Gabriel. She found some duct tape in an old toolbox. It held the diaper together.

Tye put Seth on his back and Clay carried Gabriel as they stomped through the woods to where Red and the plane waited.

"Pane?" Gabriel uttered, his eyes wide.

"You got it boy. It's an airplane and you're about to fly in the sky." Red scooped him in the air and flew him to his seat.

Gabriel's giggles lilted up and down as if on a rollercoaster of delight.

Tye strapped Seth into the space beside him. "What do you think, Seth?"

"I like the airplane," his firm tone belied his five years.

The plane tried to reach the clouds. It swooped up and down, thanks to Red's maneuvers.

Lexie sang out "wow" with each downward shift. Soon the men called out, too. Laughter came from Gabriel in quick spurts with each downward motion. Seth sat quietly, his eyes locked on the airplane's instrument panel.

Tye attempted to engage him, "Seth, what do you think of flying?"

"I want an airplane."

Red entered the conversation, "Someday, Seth Langley, I'll teach you how to fly."

"You will?" the child responded in disbelief.

"I'll hire a co-pilot in about fifteen years, and you look like the guy for me."

Seth stared out the window. His mouth turned up slightly. The darkness in his eyes lightened.

Back at the field, which Diffee called an airport, the group exited the plane. Seth trailed behind Tye.

The sudden crunch of running feet on dead grass provoked Lexie to turn. Seth ran into Red's arms for a giant swing.

"Will you really teach me how to fly an airplane when I'm big?"

"If I'm alive and well, we've got a deal. Let's shake on it." Red stretched out his arm.

The boy grasped the big hand. "It's a deal."

Chapter Two

Lexie drove the patrol car to the side of the old child welfare building. Myrna Easton walked toward the boys. Myrna was their caseworker a few months before when the parents were threatened with losing custody of the brothers. Gabriel immediately clung to her outreached hand. Seth stood back as if appraising the situation.

Myrna held her free hand out. "Don't you remember me, Seth? I know your mom and dad."

Slowly, he moved toward her.

"I'm hungry. How about you guys?" Myrna asked.

"Hunry," Gabriel repeated.

"We're off to lunch," Myrna answered. "Thanks for bringing me these sweet boys."

Lexie watched as the trio went through the double doors. "I'll never understand how anyone can leave their children alone."

Tye's voice filled with disgust. "Druggies aren't known for their good sense."

Lexie went into boss mode. "Clay, take the patrol car. Tye and I'll walk to the office from here."

Five minutes later, the pair was back in the sheriff's office. Four gray metal desks were dispersed throughout the room. Ten, unmatched, four-drawer file cabinets were lined in a row against a wall. All the furniture pieces were rejects from the city hall renovation. A flowered chair, a striped chair, and two leather chairs were in the last stages of deterioration.

As usual, Delia sat at a three-legged table in the corner using the computer. The electric machine was the only thing in the room less than two years old. The two jail cells looked like Mayberry revisited, without the charm.

A vase of yellow daffodils on Delia's desk was the only cheerful color in the room otherwise filled with brown and gray hues.

"Tye, go to lunch," Lexie instructed, "and take Delia with you."

"I'm fine. I'm fine," Delia fussed. "With the shape I'm in, I can go three months without eating and still be over two hundred pounds. Anyway, these reports aren't finished."

"Come on, Beautiful," Tye teased, "you know you want a lunch date with me."

"I might consider it if I were twenty-five years younger."

Tye's bottom lip protruded, "Another woman giving me the brush off."

Lexie flicked her hand in dismissal. "You two get out of here, so I can write notes in peace."

"Okay! Okay!" Tye headed for the door. "I'm tell everyone at Dixie's restaurant that it's easier to have a leg blown off than to have a little sister for a boss."

Alone, Lexie wondered where Wilbur went and how long he planned to leave his stepchildren alone. He'd hid his meth business in the woods for years and always avoided getting arrested. His friends and customers covered for him, but he couldn't avoid her forever. Now she had proof of his guilt, not to mention the child neglect charges. The ringing phone interrupted her thoughts.

"Sheriff Wolfe here."

"This is Detective Johnson from Lasell, Washington.

We're transporting a body for burial in your town. Woman's name is Terri Womack." His words came out rapid fire in a low masculine voice.

Lexie stammered momentarily, then went silent as she processed the shock. Tears surfaced at the awful words the voice spoke.

"Are you still there?" Johnson questioned.

"I know Terri. How did she die?"

"Murdered by her husband. Some softhearted judge decided that the accused murderer deserved to attend his wife's funeral. In case he killed her out of love, not loathing."

The sarcasm in his voice twisted Lexie's stomach into a knot. "I know her husband. They were high school sweethearts."

"Well, there's nothing sweet about them now—one dead and one in jail," Johnson scoffed. "He was a fool. She was almost dead from cancer, and he injected her with curare to finish her off fast."

"You think it was a mercy killing?"

"Regardless, it's still murder." Johnson continued, "May I keep him in your jail for two nights? I'll escort him to the funeral, then we'll be gone."

"Sure," Lexie agreed. "When can I expect you?"

"We'll arrive the day after tomorrow."

"See you then." Lexie hung up.

She dreaded Tye and Delia's reactions to the news. Ronald and Terri graduated with Tye. Delia considered every kid born in Diffee a family member.

The rattle of the office door signaled their return.

"Tye, I received a call from Washington. A Detective Johnson requested we house his prisoner, Ronald Womack."

Tye moved to the window and stared into the distance. Lexie's words followed him, "He's accused of murder—Terri's. Likely, it's a mercy killing."

Tye's voice cracked, "Ronald's no murderer. Maybe a heartbroken husband trying to stop her pain, but not a killer."

"That's right," Delia's voice squeezed out the words. "I'll never forget watching him at the County Fair showing his goats. He stood proud beside his spiffed up goats waitin' to hear who won the blue ribbon."

Tye's words shot out with a spray of saliva. "Why's Johnson bringing him here?"

"So he can attend Terri's funeral."

Tye turned from the window. "He'll feel humiliated jailed in in his home town."

"Better that," Delia disagreed, "than miss his wife's funeral. I'll bring a quilt and pillow from home for the cell cot, and cook chicken and dumplings for him."

"I'll clear up this mess!" Tye's conviction was evident.

Lexie wondered how Johnson would react to all this TLC for his accused murderer.

Chapter Three

"Hallelujah, praise the Lord!" The preacher's voice bounced off the converted barn's rafters and soaked into the sinners below.

"Hallelujah," echoed the preacher's wife, Tina, and the rest of the congregation. They called out from hard wooden benches that faced her husband and an eight-foot metal cross.

Gavin's shirtsleeves were rolled up. A circle of sweat under each arm gave evidence that the man put much energy into his work. He brushed a lock of brown hair from his forehead, then raised an arm in praise of his Maker.

"I'm not here as Gavin Smith, the man. I'm here as Gavin Smith—God's servant. He called me to preach as He called each of you to join his army of believers. LISTEN, not to your own voice, not to the voices of friends, or your boss or sinners of the world, but only to God's voice. Rise up and come forward to seek His joy, His glory, and His love." Gavin's words pulled people from their seats and they walked down aisles toward him.

Tina easily slipped out the back door. She figured she had at least a couple of hours while her husband prayed with the newly saved. She'd meet with Bud and return to the motel before Gavin finished saving souls.

"Come, if you haven't come before. Come, if you need to start over again."

I've already started over, Tina thought, as she walked toward her car. I don't want to begin again.

"COME FOLLOW JESUS! He will lead you on this

earth and when your life is done, HE WILL LEAD YOU STRAIGHT TO HEAVEN! Come forward and let me introduce you to our Savior."

Gavin's words followed her across the parking lot. The rolled up window shut out his call to sinners. She had no confessions for Gavin Smith. Driving toward the park, her only purpose was to remove Bud from her life forever. His phone call yesterday brought back old memories.

"I must talk to you," the voice said.

"Who's this?" Tina asked.

"Surely, you haven't forgotten an old friend from Diffee."

"Bud, is that you?"

"I've come a long way to see you. Let's meet tonight at Bluebird Park. Not the same as Diffee Park, but it'll bring back memories."

"I'd love to, but I can't. This is the first night of my husband's revival and I have to attend."

"You can miss one sermon for an old friend," Bud pleaded.

"No, I can't. I'm a different person now. I was saved. Memories of my past conjure up the sins I committed."

"You will meet me," he dictated.

"My past is nonexistent. I can't look back,"

"Here's the deal, my dear friend, either you meet me or I'll tell your preacher husband that he married a whore. I'll enlighten him as to why you were voted friendliest girl in your senior class."

"Why would you do that? I thought we were friends."

"Give me a few minutes, then I'll never bother you

again."

Tina yielded, "I'll arrive at nine o'clock."

Bud hung up without reply.

Better here than at home. The revival was an advantage. She didn't know anyone who could identify her at the park. After pulling in near the picnic area, she checked the locks on her car doors three times. She visually examined the wooded area that surrounded the park. A lone light cast shadows on the children's play equipment.

She was impatient for Bud's arrival even though she was early. Part of Tina wanted to see him, but over the last few hours her anger grew due to his bossiness. She resolved to tell him what she thought of his attitude. After all, she wasn't the only one who had dirty secrets.

A March night, twenty years ago, was forever imbedded in Tina's memory. Eight senior girls sat around a campfire. They ate, laughed, talked, drank beer, and celebrated the best day of their lives, the Friday before they won the Oklahoma Girls Basketball Championship.

The Diffee newspaper dubbed them the 'Extraordinary Eight' after they won their first six games of the season. They were the darlings of Diffee, Oklahoma, a small town that never had anything to cheer for before, or since, that year. The town locked up on Friday nights and everyone watched their darlings play basketball. A Tulsa television station did a segment on the Friday night, basketball ghost town. A national station picked up the story and the girls became small time celebrities. Little kids asked for their autographs and old people patted their backs and told them how proud they were. Team parents basked in the glory of having daughters who were local heroines. Tina knew she and her teammates didn't deserve the accolades. Her mind returned to the present when an approaching car spotlighted her location.

Chapter Four

The gravel crackled beneath Bud's tires as he drove into the parking area. His car lights shone on the only vehicle. As he walked toward Tina, she got out of her car and leaned against the door.

"Hello," he said.

"Hi," she replied, her anger dissolving. "You sounded hateful on the phone."

"I'm sorry, but I had to see you."

"It's okay," Tina acquiesced. "What's so important?"

Bud touched her cheek, "I came to say goodbye."

"Where are you going?"

His features stiffened. "I'm not going anywhere. You, however, are on your way to heaven or hell, depending on how forgiving your God is." His left hand took a fistful of blouse at her throat.

"Oh, God...No!" Her small fists raged against his back, then her boney knee shot up between his legs.

With his feet planted solidly on the ground, he showed no reaction to her struggles. He grabbed her arm with his left hand and stuck the needle into her forearm, releasing the curare. She collapsed. He watched her body writhe. Fingernails dug into the dirt for only seconds as her body turned blue from the loss of oxygen.

"Two down and five to go."

Chapter Five

Lexie, Tye, and Delia watched from the office window as Johnson and Ronald walked up the sidewalk. Lexie saw faces stare from the front of Dixie's restaurant, across the street.

"Goodness, why is Ronald handcuffed?" Delia nervously twisted an escaped strand of long grey hair from her bun.

Tye scowled, "He's an asshole!"

"That's enough." Lexie's glare focused on Tye. "Johnson sees Ronald as a murderer, not a good old boy from town."

Tye clamped his lips into an angry line. He stomped out the back door as Ronald and Johnson came in the front.

"I'm Stan Johnson," the detective announced.

"I'm Lexie Wolfe. This is Delia, our dispatcher and secretary."

"Here's the prisoner," Johnson squeezed Ronald's shoulder.

Ronald stood silently with downcast eyes. His body leaned forward making his bald spot the most visible part of his head.

"I know Ronald. My brother, Tye, attended high school with him."

Delia walked toward Ronald. "My dear, dear boy. I'm so sorry about Terri."

Only a sob came from Ronald's mouth, then another and another. Delia wrapped her soft-thick arms around his slender frame. His body curved over as he bent and cried on her shoulder.

"Pitiful," Johnson shook his head in disgust. "Where can

I stay in town?"

"There's a motel a mile east," Lexie answered against the background of Ronald's now quieter sobs. "I'll take over—give you a break."

"I won't leave until he's locked up."

"That's easy enough. Ronald, get in the cell," Lexie directed.

Delia held his arm and accompanied him. She patted the multi-colored quilt, and Ronald immediately lay down like an obedient puppy. "Rest here," she whispered.

Delia hesitantly left Ronald's side and Lexie closed the cell door.

Johnson pulled the door. "He's set. I'll come back at 10 a.m., sooner if you'll let me buy you breakfast."

"Nine-thirty works," Lexie responded. She felt Delia's disapproving look as Johnson walked out the door.

"That guy doesn't have a heart," Delia blurted. "Hard to believe a man that handsome is so ugly inside."

"Just doing his job," Lexie said flatly.

She didn't respond to Delia's comment about Johnson's looks. However, she was sure that she'd never, in her thirty-one years, seen a man who looked that good. He was probably five feet-ten, blond hair, green eyes, and a body that appeared in perfect physical condition. She didn't usually gawk at men, but it was difficult not to stare at Stan.

Chapter Six

The door slammed behind Tye. It rocked the old birdhouse that hung in the tree outside the office. His lips locked and his head pounded with the words he didn't say. His kid sister reprimanding him then defending some joker she didn't know, plus the news about Ronald, was too much.

He drove the patrol car back and forth on Main Street. He searched for a jaywalker or speeder on whom he could take out some of his anger. *What a joke!* His life had evaporated into vengeance against someone who didn't use a crosswalk. Every day he asked himself why he was still in Diffee. The answer remained the same—Lexie refused to go on with her life until Dad's killer was locked up. Tye was a captive to her obsession. He wondered where they'd be if it never happened. Lexie might have three kids and he'd live somewhere else. That's where he was moving after Dad's killer was caught—anywhere else. Calmed, he forced himself back to face boss sister and Ronald.

Chapter Seven

Ronald was eating chicken and dumplings when Tye returned. He reached out his hand to shake Ronald's—then got to the point. "What happened?"

"I didn't kill Terri."

"Ronald, be straight with me. I understand that a man wants to keep the people he loves from suffering."

"I told you. I didn't kill her," Ronald's voice was raspy with irritation. "As soon as I walked in the door I saw her bluish skin and yelled for help."

"Is there anyone who can verify that you walked in the room immediately prior to yelling?" Lexie questioned.

"There was a tall guy with a gray beard and toupee in the hall. He ignored me when I tried to make eye contact with him."

Lexie's brow furrowed, "Why do you remember him?"

"I was going to signal that his toupee was crooked. After he acted like a snob, I didn't care if he looked like a fool."

"That guy may be your alibi," Tye reasoned. "What room did he exit from?"

"There were half a dozen possibilities."

"Private rooms?" Lexie asked.

"Yes," Ronald nodded.

"That means he was visiting one of those six patients."

"You better not jack with us." Tye's voice went from kind to suspicious. "If you did make this man up, don't send us on a wild goose chase."

"I'm not lying. She begged to die, but I wasn't man

enough to help her. I was too selfish. Every minute she was alive was one more minute she was mine." The words came quickly out of Ronald's mouth as if to escape before emotion gagged him.

"We'll get you out of this."

Lexie grimaced at Tye's promise. She knew handsome Stan wouldn't tolerate interference in his case.

Chapter Eight

Heather thought about dying as she drove her old Jeep across the metal bridge: easy to turn the wheel sharply to the left. She saw the car in her mind, smashing through the metal barrier and diving headlights first into the river. She visualized the car sinking. Water surrounded her red hair. Each strand floated like a tentacle of blood around her head. The water crept through the windows and replaced all her oxygen. Her life, thankfully, would be over. She wondered if her cheating ex-husband's girlfriend would accompany him to the funeral.

A memory hit her brain like lightening and her words spewed out, "Oh shit, sonofabitch! I haven't removed his name from my life insurance policy. I'll be damned if he and his little whore princess will inherit fifty thousand dollars off me." Fearful that she'd tempted fate with her imaginings, she slowed down and firmly gripped the wheel.

Heather walked into Dr. William's office twenty minutes late. She flopped down on the overstuffed leather chair that faced his desk and avoided his disapproving eyes.

"Only twenty minutes left in your session, Heather. Why are you late?"

"I contemplated driving my car off a bridge."

"That's interesting. What stopped you?"

"I realized that I hadn't changed the beneficiary on my insurance. D.A. Lave has so many friends at the police department they'd call it an accident instead of a suicide in order to fill his wallet."

"A psychiatrist appears incompetent if a patient commits suicide." He nervously pressed his hand across his mouth. It covered his mustache and disrupted the perfect grooming of his beard.

"It's nothing personal, Doc. It's not your fault I hit the peak of my life at eighteen. My senior year I was homecoming queen, class president and an outstanding basketball player. Since then, everything I touch turns to shit."

Dr. Williams crossed his arms in front of his chest. "How do I know you won't hurt yourself tonight?"

"My insurance agent is on vacation. I can't change the policy for a week."

"STOP joking about suicide, Heather. You're a beautiful and bright woman. Why are you allowing that fool of an ex-husband to ruin your life?"

"I wasn't good enough. He replaced me with a younger model."

"That's incorrect, Heather. *He* wasn't good enough. If a woman like you loved me, I'd treasure her." Moisture clouded his eyes.

"Doc...Paul, I'm sorry. I didn't mean to upset you."

"Heather, I can't continue as your therapist."

"You're deserting me, too?"

His elbows bent on his desk. His hands massaged his forehead. "I can't deal with your problems professionally. I've fallen in love with you."

"Paul, I don't know what to say."

"I require a promise that you'll go inpatient for a month. I asked Dr. Lowery to take over your case."

"It'll take me a couple of days to get everything in order.

You know—the cat, the mail, and the life insurance policy."

"Can I trust you to phone if depression overwhelms you?"

"If a man like you can love me, then I must not be a dud after all." She craved a hug, but he didn't move from behind his desk, obviously embarrassed by his confession. She touched his hand and whispered, "I promise."

She drove her car slowly, and purposely, to her apartment.

*****

Heather awoke the next morning with a certainty she hadn't felt in months; she wanted to live. The ringing of the phone interrupted her packing.

"Heather, it's Bud."

"Bud, good grief! Talk about ancient history. What are you up to?" Heather found one empty spot on her bed and sank into it.

"I'm in town for the day and I'm on my way to visit you. After all, I haven't bugged you in twenty years."

Heather laughed, "In that case, I can spare the time. My address is 403 SW Expressway. Can you come this morning? I'm leaving on a trip tomorrow and have lots to do."

"I'll be right there."

She fell back on her mess and stared at the ceiling. Something about reliving teenage memories made her feel special. Those really were her good old days.

She phoned Paul to ease his mind.

"I'm with a patient. Please leave a message."

"Paul, it's Heather. I'm fine and getting packed. An old friend from high school is dropping by this morning. I'm so excited! I'll talk to you soon."

Bud knocked on Heather's door fifteen minutes later.

"You're quick," she chatted. "Most people get lost three times before they find my place."

"I have great directionality."

"Come in, stranger," Heather welcomed. "It's good to see you."

"I heard you've had some tough times." Bud's words sounded accusatory.

"Sounds like I'm still on the gossip line."

"Sorry to upset you."

"You're not. I've had failures—even failed at committing suicide—twice. That should be the definition of a loser." Heather smiled.

"I'll assist you," Bud offered.

"No thanks. Today I'm the best I've been in years."

Bud's face went blank. "I don't want to help you live. I want to help you die."

"My psychiatrist griped at me for making jokes about death. He's right. It's morbid. Let's change the subject."

"Your death is the only subject I'm interested in."

"Cut it out! You're not funny." Heather stood, her hands firmly planted on her hips. "Time to run my errands, so leave."

He wrapped his arms around her. Chills invaded her body from the creepy loose caress. She backed up. His grip immediately tightened. He plunged the needle into her arm. One brief scream, then her mouth froze.

*****

Bud hated it when the saliva spilled from her mouth. Seeing her turn blue was enjoyable, because it meant the poison paralyzed her lungs. He filled the tub with water, then pulled Heather's body into the bathroom. He removed his leather gloves and forced her body face down into the water.

He cocked her head to the side and stared into the darkness of her eyes. "Congratulations, Heather, you're finally a success. Me, too. Three down and four to go."

Chapter Nine

Lexie waited for Tye on the sidewalk outside the office door.

"Are you my welcoming committee?"

"We need a private conversation." Lexie continued, "I know you want to investigate Ronald's case, but we don't have jurisdiction. Even if we did have the right to interfere, we can't investigate out of state. I'll talk to Stan. He'll decide as to whether or not he pursues the leads."

"So now Detective Johnson is Stan. Well, Sheriff, I hope you convince Johnson, because if you can't, an innocent man will rot in prison. His ten-year-old son is left without a father and a mother." Avoiding a response, he turned and walked into the office.

"Lexie," a masculine voice called from across the street, "are you ready for breakfast?"

Lexie answered with a wave.

Two elderly men sat on a bench outside the restaurant. They eyed Stan and Lexie as they walked the short path to the brown rock building.

"How are you doing today?" She asked the pair.

"My arthritis always acts up on these cold damp days," Ruben complained.

"I'm okay," Sam responded. "Sad day for the town."

"Sure is sad," Ruben added, his eyes squinted at Stan. "You know that boy Ronald ain't no murderer."

"I don't know that," Stan retorted then moved toward the steps with Lexie trailing behind.

The restaurant was half full of residents dressed in dark

church clothes, obviously stopping for breakfast before Terri's funeral. The chatter in the room subsided when she and Stan entered. She made herself speak or nod to patrons as she walked toward an empty booth in the far corner of the restaurant.

It felt like a magnifying glass was focused on her. She hadn't worn a dress since she came back to run for sheriff. *Maybe some of them have enough sense to realize I'm attending a funeral. Gossips will say I tried to impress the hunk of a detective.* The thought irritated her. After she ordered breakfast, she went into sheriff mode.

"I interviewed Ronald last night, and I think he's innocent."

"Your objectivity is questionable since he's a hometown boy."

"I barely knew him and even if I did, I wouldn't let it influence my judgment."

"What did he tell you?" Stan took a gulp of coffee.

"That he walked into Terri's hospital room and immediately yelled 'help.' There was a man in the hall. He can verify it was a matter of seconds between Ronald passing him in the hall and the yells. He described the guy as a tall man with a gray toupee and beard."

"A mysterious man is his alibi. Let me guess, Ronald doesn't know who this guy is."

"True." Lexie ignored his cynical tone. She took a bite of eggs to keep from telling him his attitude sucked.

"I don't have time to chase imaginary witnesses." Stan pointed his slice of bacon at her. "Your guy left the syringe in the sharps container. Don't you think an earlier killer would've taken the evidence with him?"

"Not necessarily, he would've immediately been implicated if he was caught with the syringe in his possession."

"When I get back, I'll interview the hospital staff, and find out if they saw Ronald's mystery man." He looked directly into her eyes, "I'm doing this to ease your mind, not because I think he's innocent."

Lexie's gaze moved to the red-gingham tablecloth. "I appreciate you doing it regardless of your reason."

"It's time to get the prisoner," he said abruptly.

"I'll put a deputy at each door of the church so he won't need handcuffs." Lexie said the words with authority, but she looked at the ruffled curtain instead of Stan's face. She didn't know if his lack of response meant he agreed, or was ready to put up a fight.

Back at her office, they found Ronald wearing a suit and tie, sitting in an open cell, talking to Clay, Tye and Delia.

"Where's the prison uniform?" Stan's irritation was evident.

"In the john," Tye answered loudly.

Ronald interrupted the verbal sparring, "Delia borrowed a suit for me."

"The pants are a little short, but the best I could find on short notice."

"How sweet!" Venom oozed from Stan's voice.

Lexie spouted out directions, "Clay, you answer the phone while we're gone so Delia can attend the funeral; Tye, stand by the church's front door; I'll stay posted by the back door; Detective Johnson will sit in the pew behind Ronald."

Johnson added his orders to Lexie's, "As soon as the funeral ends, I'll bring the prisoner back to change clothes and we'll leave. No graveyard visit or family dinner for this murderer."

Lexie nodded. She wanted to argue the point, but at least Johnson allowed Ronald to go without the handcuffs, which was just short of a miracle.

Chapter Ten

Jamie flung her pinstriped jacket on the recliner and rolled up her shirtsleeves. She propped herself against the throw pillows on Abbey's flowered sofa with her shoeless feet planted on the table's edge. "Don't you think Terri looked a little pale and stiff?"

Loretta shook her head in exasperation. "Well, shit! What do you expect from a dead person?"

"Not a hell of a lot, but you'd think that the funeral could've commenced before the body corroded."

Beth clutched a throw pillow as she spoke. "Delia told me that Terri's death is under investigation." Everything Beth wore was black, which was in distinct contrast to her light skin and prematurely white hair. "The police think that Ronald killed her to end the suffering."

"You're a regular volume of information," Jamie snipped.

"Why does Beth know this stuff, Jamie, and you don't? Perhaps you and Tye should stop during your sleepovers and have pillow talk," Loretta teased.

Abbey listened to the conversation from her kitchen. She was glad to have lunch prep as an excuse to avoid the gossip. Gary took their kids to his parents so the friends could have time alone to deal with Terri's death.

Abbey doubted that Jamie, the basketball coach; Beth, the porcelain doll; Loretta, the social climber; and herself, farm mom, would ever have become friends if their championship basketball team hadn't linked them forever. She didn't know if she could handle spending over two hours with *the boss, the bitch,* and *the meek.* Gary agreed to come home at 2 p.m. to cue the women to leave.

Nothing motivated Loretta to move faster than a toddler wanting to sit on her lap, or a little hand reaching toward her perfectly styled blonde hair. Nicky had run Loretta off in the past and Abbey's little wild boy could do it again, if his services were required.

Abbey was surprised Loretta showed up after the funeral. She hesitated when invited.

'At your farm?' Her tone was acid. 'I guess I'll come if you'll keep your animals away from me.'

'I'm sure we can find a fenced-in area for you," Gary inserted.

'Didn't you redecorate? I'd love to see what you've done with your little house?' Loretta added, after a piercing look at Gary.

Abbey stabbed the tomato and began slicing it viciously at the memory.

Beth joined Abbey in the kitchen, "What can I do?"

"Tell them lunch is ready."

Jamie admired the bay window as she walked into the kitchen. "I love the new window. Did Gary put it in?"

"Yes, the man can build anything."

"It's sweet with the white ruffled curtain." Loretta pushed the panels apart. "Blinds give more light. They're so stylish now."

"I think it looks perfect," Beth said.

"No offense, dear, but style has never been your forte," Loretta scowled.

Abbey hoped to get Loretta out of bitch mode by

changing the subject. "Let's do something to honor Terri."

Jamie managed one word between bites, "What?"

"Something related to basketball since that was her claim to fame in Diffee."

"A gift to the town?" Beth suggested.

"All our names should be on a gift. She didn't win that championship by herself," Loretta grumbled as she spooned sandwich components into separate piles on her plate.

Jamie's voice warbled, "I've got it! Let's have a fundraiser and use the money to renovate the inside of the old gym—new paint, bleachers, and refinish the floor. If the superintendent agrees, we'll call it the 'Terri Womack Memorial Gymnasium.'"

Beth chimed in, "We can play a basketball game as part of our twentieth high school reunion. That way we'll raise more money. 'Killing two birds with one stone' as the old people say."

"Beth, stay away from old people if they're repeating weird things about birds."

Jamie curled her lip at Loretta.

Abbey ignored the pair. "Who will we play?"

"How about Jamie's college team? She can make them take a fall for us." Loretta raised her eyebrows in anticipation of Jamie's reaction.

"Not in this lifetime, my girls aren't taking a fall for anyone."

"Keep in mind," Abbey added, "It's twenty years later and I'm fifteen pounds heavier. We want to find a team that's not good."

Jamie laughed, "The nursing home doesn't have a team."

Abbey stuck out her tongue.

Loretta fluffed her hair, "The high school team is lousy. Let's play them."

"Beth, since you teach at the high school, will you ask the superintendent?" Abbey continued, "I'll phone Tina, Mariah, and Heather and talk them into playing."

"I bet Mariah won't come. Rumors are circulating that her war hero husband is the dark horse for the Republican presidential nomination."

"Wow, Beth! Think of the money we'd collect if the wife of a candidate played." Abbey's eyes brightened at the prospect.

Loretta shook her head, "No way will someone of Mariah's stature make a spectacle of herself. Not sure if I'll do it either."

Racket from the front porch signaled Abbey that her family was about to save her from a dismal conversation.

"Things to do." Loretta stood as Nicky made a beeline for her lap. He grabbed a leg and hung as she walked toward the door. Gary unclasped his giggling son from the irate woman.

"Teach that boy self-control," Loretta panted.

Gary followed her out to the porch. "Kids aren't grown-up by thirteen months."

Loretta made a noise that sounded like a ferocious animal and stomped to her BMW.

"I'll make calls in the morning," Abbey promised Beth and Jamie after their goodbye hugs.

"Gary, there's nothing like spending a couple of hours with my teammates to remind me how lucky I am to have you and the kids."

"If I'm so damn wonderful, give me a big smooch?" Gary puckered his lips like a fish. Abbey grabbed him around the neck and planted a long kiss firmly on his lips.

Chapter Eleven

Abbey pushed aside the breakfast dishes and started her *to do* list. The sun from the bay window left streaks of light on her short, brown curls. She wore her favorite clothes—old sweatpants with a T-shirt. Her bare feet touched something sticky under the table. "Oh, the joy of motherhood."

"What'd you say?" Gary hollered from the family room.

"I have sticky toes from your little guy dropping jelly on the floor. I'll scrub the floor for the second time this week."

Gary leaned against the door facing, "If you wore shoes you wouldn't feel the jelly."

"Sounds like male logic to me."

He wrapped his arms around her, "That's the best kind."

"You go do man stuff. I have a basketball game to organize."

"Yes, my queen."

"I like the sound of that," Abbey laughed.

She dialed Heather's phone number. "May I speak to Heather?"

"Who's this?"

"I'm Abbey King. I went to high school with Heather.

"This is Heather's dad."

"Mr. Hobart, it's been a long time."

"I'm moving Heather's stuff out of her apartment. She died."

"Died?" Abbey gasped.

"Heather attempted suicide twice last year and managed to survive. This time she succeeded. She was found dead in her bathtub." His voice cracked, "I can't believe that she's gone."

"I'm so sorry, Mr. Hobart. Is there anything I can do?"

"It's too late. I can't talk anymore." His voice deteriorated to a whimper and the phone clicked.

Light rays made jagged marks across the wall. She wished for rain with lightning and thunder. A loud racket to interrupt the living so the world would know her friend died. Instead, Heather's passing was diminished by the cheerful glare of the sun.

Heather chose to die, Abbey reasoned, now she has her peace. She cried softly for a few minutes then forced herself back to the phone

Next task—phone Sean Haverty, Mariah's dad, to ask for her number. "Sean, it's Abbey. Please give me Mariah's phone number. I want to invite her to play a benefit basketball game with our old team."

He rattled off the number.

"Are you okay?" Abbey asked. "I heard about your heart problems."

"I'm fine. My old ticker slowed down—like the rest of me."

"Take care of yourself, Sean. I'll see you at church tomorrow. Goodbye."

Mariah's phone rang six times before a man answered, "Toleson residence."

"May I speak to Mariah, please?"

"Who should I say is calling?"

"Abbey King, a high school friend."

"Are you sure you're not a reporter? I've heard similar tricks."

"I'm the real deal. We played on a basketball team together."

"I've been Mrs. Toleson's personal assistant for three years. She's never once mentioned basketball. I'll take your number so she can return your call, if she chooses."

"Okay," Abbey responded.

One roadblock after another, was her thought as she dialed Sean again.

"Sean, Mariah's assistant didn't let me talk to her. He thinks I'm a reporter. Will you phone and tell her about the game?"

Sean agreed.

Abbey dialed the last number on her list.

"May I speak to Tina?"

"Mom died," a child's voice squeaked. "Talk to my Dad."

Abbey suppressed the moan that was rising from her throat.

"Hello," said a somber voice.

"I went to high school with Tina. How did she die?" Abbey's voice cracked every couple of words. She wasn't sure she made sense.

"Who are you?"

"Abbey King. I played basketball on the Diffee High School team with Tina."

"I do remember her mentioning your name," Gavin spoke slowly. "She died of respiratory failure as a result of poisoning. She was murdered."

"Did they arrest her killer?"

"No."

"I'm...sorry for your loss!"

"Thank you," strained from his throat. Then the phone went dead.

She clutched her trembling hands. "Gary!" she cried out.

He ran into the kitchen. "My God, what's wrong?"

"My friends are dead," she moaned.

"Who's dead?"

"Heather and Tina are dead like Terri!"

He wrapped his arms around her and held tight. Her body trembled in his arms as she wept. Red streaks accented her pale skin and her eyes were swelling shut.

Chapter Twelve

Abbey tried to remember how she ended up on her bed. She vaguely recalled a sensation of being picked up and carried. She didn't have a clue as to how she managed to fall asleep with all the sorrow that surrounded her. Her body felt heavy and she didn't want to leave the mattress support or the comforting darkness.

Her thoughts returned to the discovery of a bizarre series of deaths that resulted in the loss of three good friends. *It can't be. It doesn't make any sense, unless....*Her body shuddered as if a cold wind suddenly came through the window. She pulled the receiver off the nightstand phone and pressed 9-1-1. The base of the phone fell and dangled from the short cord.

Abbey's voice quivered, "Delia, get Lexie."

"She's right here."

Abbey heard Delia whisper, "It's Abbey. She sounds upset."

"Hello."

"Lexie, something's terribly wrong. Heather and Tina are both dead. I think someone is killing the members of our basketball team. Three out of the eight died within a two week period." Abbey's words came out in rapid sequence. She clinched the phone with her right hand and her head with her left.

"How did Tina and Heather die?"

Abbey heard the suppressed shock in Lexie's voice.

"Tina was murdered in a park and Heather was drowned

in her bathtub. Heather's dad said it was a suicide. What if it wasn't? You didn't think Ronald murdered Terri, so someone else did. Tina's murderer wasn't arrested." Abbey couldn't contain the speed of her words. It was as if she had to tell Lexie fast, before another horrible thing happened.

"I know you're upset, Abbey. But it's a long stretch from three women dying to someone targeting an entire team. Terri's death looks like a mercy killing, and I heard that Heather attempted suicide last year. It doesn't make any sense that someone is killing eight teenage girls twenty years later."

"Can't you investigate?" Abbey attempted to sound calm.

"No, I can't. Even if I thought there was reason for suspicion, these cases are out of my jurisdiction."

"Okay," Abbey said with uncertainty. "It's bizarre that they died so close to each other."

"I know," Lexie sympathized, "I'm sorry that you lost three good friends."

Abbey hung up without saying goodbye.

She turned to Gary, "Lexie won't do anything. She thinks it's a coincidence."

"It may be," Gary shrugged, "why don't you let it go?"

Her body stiffened. "I won't chance that someone may die because I didn't warn them."

"You may scare them for no reason." Gary held her hand.

She jerked it away, "You think I'm crazy! Don't you?"

"I think you're upset. If you'll feel better after you phone and warn your friends—then do it. They can accept what you say or not."

Jamie's answering machine picked up. "It's Abbey. We need to talk. Meet me in front of the library at three this afternoon."

"Hello," Loretta answered.

"Loretta, it's Abbey. Something important has come up. Meet me in front of the library at three."

"Sounds mysterious, but I'm attending a dinner party tonight. Hair and nail appointments are this afternoon."

"It may be a matter of life and death." Abbey's voice squeaked out the word *death*.

"Calm down girl. I'll manage to get there."

Beth answered the phone on the first ring, "Hello."

"Be in front of the library at three o'clock."

"What's wrong, Abbey? You sound upset."

"I'm okay. Please meet me."

"I'll be there," Beth agreed.

The personal assistant answered at Mariah's number. "This is Abbey King. It's urgent that I speak to Mariah."

"It's always an emergency when someone wants Mrs. Toleson's attention. She's not in and I assume she didn't return your last call. That's a clue that she doesn't want to talk to you."

"Rudeness is unnecessary," Abbey's tone was sharp. "What's your name? Mariah needs to know how obnoxious you are." *Even I can be a bitch if pushed to the limit.*

"My name is Wade Cartwright. Spill your guts—if she ever calls you back."

Abbey slammed the phone and started crying all over again.

After she calmed, she dialed Sean's number. "Mr. Haverty, it's Abbey. I know what I'm about to say sounds strange, but I need to get a message to Mariah. Three of her friends died suspiciously and I'm afraid she may be in danger."

"What're you talking about?" The old man wheezed out the words.

"Tina was murdered in a park, Terri was killed in the hospital, and Heather was found dead in her bathtub."

"I heard Terri's death was a mercy killing," Sean said.

"I know what they're saying," Abbey responded. "I'm afraid they're wrong."

"Did you call the sheriff about this?"

"I did, but Lexie said there wasn't proof of a connection between the deaths. She can't go out of Oklahoma to investigate anyway."

Sean's voice turned accusatory, "Well, if Lexie says there's nothing to worry about, I'll trust her opinion. It sounds like you're overreacting. Calm down and don't upset folks."

"Yes. Okay. Sorry I bothered you! Goodbye." *He put me in my place. I'll shut up before someone else thinks I've gone nuts.*

Thanks to Sean's reprimand, she felt like a fool telling Jamie, Beth, and Loretta her fears. Engulfed in thought on the drive, she arrived ten minutes late. Loretta walked toward her car.

"Come back, Loretta," Jamie called. "The secretive woman has arrived."

"I don't have time for Abbey's drama. I messed up my nails. Because of her, I left the salon before they dried; now I have to go back." She waved her chipped nail inches from Abbey's face.

Beth's eyes searched Abbey's. "What's wrong?"

"Probably nothing."

Loretta pointed a finger. "You ruined my day for 'probably nothing.'"

"Good grief," Jamie's nostrils flared, "a chip in your fingernail polish is hardly a reason to have a fit!"

Abbey stared at the crack in the sidewalk. "Heather and Tina are both dead."

"Oh, no," Beth whimpered.

"How did they die?" Jamie wrapped an arm around Abbey.

"Tina was murdered and they think Heather committed suicide."

"They're too young to die." Loretta's red lipstick was a stark contrast to her whitening face. "They're the same age I am."

"I think it's strange they died so close together. I don't want to frighten you, but I'm afraid the deaths are connected."

"Connected? What do you mean?" Loretta's body trembled as if jarred by the loudness of her own words.

"I think someone is killing off our old team."

"Good Lord, Abbey, that's ridiculous," Jamie scoffed. "All these deaths have lowered your IQ."

"No one has reason to kill me," Beth's logic was directed toward the sky, "I'm good to everyone."

Jamie tugged her arm. "You think someone has reason to kill the rest of us?"

"I didn't say that," Beth responded.

"Well, you implied it." Loretta's nostrils flared.

Tears flooded Abbey's face. "I had no intention of starting a fight. I felt you should be warned."

They each returned Abbey's goodbye hug in silence. The

three stood together as her truck passed them. She was sure they gossiped about their crazy friend's delusions.

Chapter Thirteen

Lexie kicked the quilt off and stared at the ceiling. She glanced at the clock and watched the hands move to midnight. How she longed for the sleep that refused to come. She knew why her body was on alert—guilt. Abbey's strained voice and fear ate at Lexie's brain. She dismissed her during the phone conversation, but what if Abbey was correct?

I might as well get up and do something. First, she opened the window a foot. The fresh smell flowed in from the recent thunderstorm. Next, she vacuumed the multi-color, braided rug in her living room. Then she fluffed the red throw pillows from the sofa and chair.

As she dusted the window shades in her bedroom, she remembered telling Delia, two years ago, that it was time to buy a new bedspread with matching drapes. Instead, the worn quilt bought at a garage sale was still her only bed covering. The window shades were yellowed from age and the sun.

After an hour she crawled back into bed. Her body, heavy from tiredness, sank into a deep sleep. The nightmare came as it generally did, but this time, amid the terror and blood from her father's death, there was an intermittent persistent noise.

Lexie awoke abruptly. Her brain muddled by sleep, it took a minute before she realized the phone was ringing.

"Yes," she answered.

"Gary King phoned in a panic. He said that Abbey left four hours ago to meet a friend and still hasn't come home."

Clay's voice was loud and fast as he conveyed his message.

"I'll go right there." Lexie's heart pounded. Sweat formed on her forehead. She leaned over the kitchen sink and splashed water on her face. She told herself to pull it together. *Abbey's all right. It's a freak coincidence.* She put on her uniform, then pulled her hair into a ponytail.

Thirty minutes later she arrived at the King farm. A pole light illuminated Gary, Megan, and Abbey's parents standing in the front yard. Gary met her halfway. Fear sent tremors through his body. Eruptions forced his right eye to twitch. His nostrils flared and mouth twisted. "You know she thought she was in danger. You didn't believe her. Now she's disappeared."

"I didn't investigate because her fear wasn't logical. We shouldn't assume the worse. Maybe she's okay."

"Maybe? Maybe I have a wife? Maybe my children still have a mother?"

Lexie ignored his outburst. "Did she say where she was going last night?"

"She told me to watch Nicky and Travis because she was meeting a friend," Megan stuttered. "It was a woman's voice on the phone."

"Did she say who? Where?"

"She was in a big hurry. I was watching television." Megan's body trembled. "You'd know where to find her if I'd asked."

"It's not your fault honey." The Grandmother's arms encircled Megan. "She should've left your dad a note."

Lexie questioned, "Who have you phoned?"

"Everyone," Abbey's dad interjected. "No one has seen her since she left home last night."

"I'll get a search team together. Give me the color of her vehicle and the..." Her buzzing cell phone interrupted her words.

Tye's voice was grave, "We got a call from Wilbur Langley. He found a woman's body in the woods."

The suffocating pressure originated in Lexie's chest then crept into her head. Moisture formed on her body as terror gripped her entire being.

"I went to the scene," Tye stammered. "Abbey is dead."

"I'll be right there." Lexie's skin tone blended perfectly with the scar on her face.

Gary saw her reaction and sank to the ground. "Oh, God, no. Not my Abbey."

"I'm so sorry." She stumbled toward her car.

Lexie pressed her hand against the patrol car as she walked around to the driver's side. The door handle provided her support as she vomited. Wiping her soiled mouth with her sleeve, she crawled into the seat and started the engine.

She glanced at her rearview mirror and saw Gary, Megan, and the Grandparents holding each other. The cries from Abbey's mother pierced through the car windows.

Chapter Fourteen

Lexie was suspended in disbelief. *It's so wrong, so cruel. It can't be true.* She arrived at the site without any awareness of how. Clay and Tye taped off a large area around a petite body.

Tye approached as she got out of the car. He wore his blank man face. His facade didn't let emotion invade his voice or actions. His eyes conveyed no light from within. "We got nothing but a strangled woman." He stomped his mud caked feet. "The rain soaked everything."

Tye didn't say Abbey's name. Better to pretend she wasn't his friend since kindergarten. *Maybe I should make believe, too.* But Lexie didn't have enough imagination to convince herself that she didn't cause Abbey's death.

They walked toward Abbey's body. Lexie forced herself to think about the murder investigation. If she thought about Abbey, she'd fall into an emotional dungeon. She'd be alone in the darkness, which sounded appealing. If she went there, however, she'd never find a way out.

"She wasn't killed here," Lexie concluded as she pulled on gloves.

"What?" Clay sounded confused.

"There's a drag path across the dirt. Look at her shirt and back of her jeans. They're encrusted with damp dirt and rock. Someone dumped her then dragged her."

Clay rubbed his forehead. "I can't imagine why the killer moved the body."

"He didn't want evidence collected at the actual scene,"

Lexie answered.

"We've combed the entire area," Tye reported. "There's no sign of her car." He still didn't say her name.

"I followed the four-wheeler tracks toward the creek," Clay pointed, as if she could actually see the area he talked about. "Tracks ended where the dirt meets the rocks on the riverbank. Whoever it was, stayed on the rocks."

"You and Tye return to where the tracks ended. Go in opposite directions, and see if you can find where the tracks pick up. He can't have stayed on the bank forever."

"You think he drove the thing in the water?"

"That's a possibility," Lexie answered. "Take flashlights so you'll have better visibility."

Lexie knelt next to the body and visually searched for any clues. Abbey's hair and clothes were soaked. Lexie took samples from under Abbey's fingernails and in her mouth. She removed particles, hairs, and anything else from the body that the murderer might have left. Photos were shot from every angle. She also made prints of the four-wheeler tracks. The culprit smoothed over areas in the dirt where his shoeprints were.

Clay and Tye returned an hour later. "Nothing either way," Tye reported in a monotone.

Clay suppressed a yawn. "As far as I'm concerned, he pushed the thing into the water."

"We'll get divers to check the lake tomorrow," Lexie commented.

After four hours of initial investigation, highway patrol officers transported the body and evidence to the Oklahoma State Bureau of Investigation in Tulsa.

"First thing in the morning, Tye, call in divers. Also, ask

Red to fly you over the entire lake area to search for Abbey's car," Lexie directed.

"You two go home and get some rest. Clay, take care of our regular duties while Tye and I concentrate on this."

Clay's feet drug as he walked toward his patrol car.

"Are you headed home, Sis?"

"I'll warn the others."

"I'll go with you," Tye's voice was uncharacteristically gentle.

"No. It's my duty."

He squeezed her arm.

She drove down the dark road behind his truck. Her unforgiveable mistake would soon be revealed to Beth, Jamie, and Loretta.

Lexie banged on Beth's door at 6 a.m. Her husband, Darren, stood shirtless behind the screen. His chest heaved and the few hairs on it were moist.

"For God's sake, you scared us to death."

Lexie's eyes and Darren's were at the same level. "There's an emergency."

Beth walked up beside Darren. Her hands wrenched as she stared at Lexie, "Come in."

Lexie stopped in the entry. "Your life is in danger, Beth. Someone is murdering members of your old basketball team."

"That's what Abbey thought. She said you didn't believe her."

"I was wrong."

"Why did you change your mind?"

Lexie blurted, "Abbey was murdered last night."

Beth's body moved in slow motion toward the floor.

Darren's arms interrupted her downward descent. He gently picked her up and laid her on the sofa.

Lexie ran to the bathroom for a damp towel.

Darren wiped the end of the cloth across Beth's forehead and down her cheeks as Lexie watched. After a couple of minutes, Beth opened her eyes.

"It can't be true," she whispered.

"I'm sorry." Lexie knew she'd say the same powerless words over and over.

"Abbey is the best person I know," Beth whimpered. "There was no reason to hurt her."

"But someone killed her." Lexie felt the sympathy drain from her body as the tough investigator took over. "Who'd want to murder members of your old team?"

"No one. We were kids."

"Who got angry at you? Who was jealous? What happened that made someone angry enough to kill?" Lexie fired the questions at the pallid woman lying listlessly on the sofa.

Darren intervened, " Back off, can't you see she's in shock?"

"Don't let her out of your sight," she ordered over her shoulder. The screen door banged in her wake.

Fifteen minutes later, Lexie formed her hands into fists and attacked Jamie's front door. After five minutes and no answer, she pounded on the back door.

Moisture formed on her body and her hands shook. *Maybe the killer got to Jamie.* She pulled out her gun and aimed the handle toward the door window.

"STOP! What the hell are you doing?" Jamie screeched as she pulled the door open.

Lexie's voice tensed with irritation and fear. "I'm trying to find out if you're alive or dead."

Jamie's spit sprinkled Lexie's face, "You scared the crap out of me."

"Someone wants you dead."

"What?"

"Abbey was right. Someone is killing your team members. She was murdered last night."

"Abbey? Murdered?"

"Yes."

Jamie's voice filled with venom. "You have a strange way of breaking the news!"

"There's no time for subtlety. You're in danger."

"I got the message, LEAVE."

"Tell me what you girls did that made someone want you all dead?"

"What did we do?" Jamie clenched her fists. "You think we were a team of demons who generated enough hate that we provoked someone to murder?"

"I'm not blaming anyone. My job is to figure out why this happened. Who would do this?"

"There wasn't anyone and, as I said earlier, you can leave."

Jamie followed her to the back door. Lexie turned to ask another question as the door slammed behind her. She watched as a crack appeared in the glass and curved upward.

Back in the patrol car, Lexie drove toward Loretta's house. The front door was open when she arrived. She held the door ajar and called, "Loretta?"

"I'm here," she answered. Loretta sat on her blue velvet sofa. She wore a perfectly coordinated gown, robe, and house shoes of pink satin. Her blonde hair was tied back with a pink ribbon. Her husband wasn't present.

"You know?" Lexie asked.

"Jamie warned me that psycho-sheriff was on the loose."

"Who do you think murdered your friends?" Lexie commanded.

"We didn't do anything to die for. There were plenty of girls jealous of Heather and me. We were the two prettiest girls in the school. People were irritated by Terri's caustic remarks and Mariah's snobbishness. Jamie bossed everyone. The other two, Beth and Abbey, were goody-goody. Hardly a group that'd bring out the killer instinct—especially twenty years later."

"Yet something has—one of you must know something even if you don't realize it. Think this through."

"I already told you—I don't know. If you'd listened to Abbey, she wouldn't be dead." Loretta's lips parted slightly. She looked at Lexie with an unblinking stare. "It's your job to figure this out Sheriff, not mine."

"Never be alone." Lexie forced authority into her words and demeanor. "The next one may be you."

"My chances for survival aren't looking good with you handling the case," Loretta chided.

Lexie locked the door on the way out. She drove her vehicle toward the lake. Perhaps in the light of day she'd find something that would lead to Abbey's killer.

She didn't feel sleepy. Her body was hypervigilant and her brain played the previous hours over and over. It was like a horror movie without an end and she was the evil monster.

Chapter Fifteen

Delia rose when Tye entered the sheriff's office. "Where's Lexie?"

"I haven't seen her since we investigated the murder site early this morning. I thought she'd be here," Tye answered.

"I haven't heard a word from her. She didn't answer her cell phone or her radio. Clay hasn't seen her either. He said that Lexie was taking Abbey's death really hard. Is that right?"

Tye nodded, "Any calls about the murder?"

"At least nine—all of them angry with Lexie. One said she didn't have any business being sheriff. Another guy shouted that she caused Abbey's death. One woman hoped Lexie would come to the same end. I'm afraid one of those lunatics will hurt her. She shouldn't be runnin' around by herself." Delia patted her white cotton hanky under each eye.

Tye placed an arm around her. "Remember, our girl has a gun, and she can blow a cap off of a bottle. I know, because she smashed my beer bottles perfecting her shot."

Delia added a subdued laugh to Tye's loud one.

"Anyone call with tips on who killed Abbey?"

Delia shook her head, "No help, only hate."

Tye glanced at his sister's cracked leather chair and headed out the door.

Chapter Sixteen

Somewhere, there's a forest that doesn't have faces of sad children in the trees and the wind doesn't moan. Somewhere there is a lake full of raindrops—not tears. Somewhere there's a mother alive instead of outlined on the ground where her dead body fell.

Lexie returned to the murder scene. Sad thoughts whirled around her head as she resolved to resign as sheriff. She'd pack everything she owned in her Jeep. She'd drive somewhere and never come back.

"Slacking off, Sheriff Wolfe?" Tye called as he walked across the grass.

"Studying the crime scene."

"You should have it memorized by now. Let's get something to eat."

"I'm not hungry."

"You planning on staying in these woods the rest of your life?"

"Only for a day or two," Lexie paused. "Then I'll move on."

Tye scowled, "That means...what?"

"I can't stay in Diffee. They all hate me. Even if they don't tell me with words, their eyes show me. Everyone blames me for Abbey's death and they're right. I ignored her fears and she ended up dead."

"You can't kill people by ignoring them," Tye scoffed.

"Don't be a smartass. I had a chance to save her and I didn't."

"Impossible to save someone who went to the woods after dark, when she thought her life was in danger."

"She trusted the person who phoned her. Abbey wasn't stupid."

"The last thing she ever did was stupid," Tye countered.

"I'm sure you're trying to make me feel better in your own crude way. Putting down Abbey doesn't alleviate my guilt."

"The only one who should feel bad is the one who killed her and we're going to get him."

"I'm not getting anyone. I'm finished here." Lexie's eyes focused on the spot where Abbey was found.

"Like hell you are little sister. You got me in this deputy business. You convinced me we had to find Dad's killer. Now we have two murderers to apprehend. We don't have time for a pity party."

"I can't bear to face them."

"You've got two days to toughen up."

"For what?"

"Abbey's funeral."

Lexie's voice quivered, "No, I can't."

"We'll pay our last respects," Tye said with certainty, "not to mention the need to look for suspicious mourners."

"Shush." Lexie's finger touched her lips, and her right hand pointed west.

Tye flattened his ear on the ground. "Someone, or something, is coming this way."

Lexie formed her hands into a stirrup and boosted Tye into an oak tree. He reached down and pulled her into the branches. Climbing trees when they were young was beneficial. Then, as now, they looked for bad guys and wild animals. They weren't pretending anymore.

The siblings were so still that a sparrow sat on a branch within a foot of Lexie's hand. Its little head cocked left, then right. Two voices got louder as seconds passed. Lexie felt as calm as the bird looked. Whoever was coming was nothing compared to what she already faced.

Now that she knew the visitors were human, she slipped down and left Tye camouflaged in the leaves. She knelt behind a boulder. The rough surface pressed against her skin. The voices came closer. Their sounds mingled with the rustling leaves and chirping birds.

Her glance scanned the area, then rested on a white streak visible through a cluster of trees. The patrol car might clue the visitors to their presence. She crawled from her hideout and got a glimpse of two men a few yards away.

Wilbur pointed, "What the hell is on the other side of those trees?"

"Shit, it's a cop car!" Toby swung around, "I's gettin' out of here!"

Lexie stepped forward and leveled her gun at the cousins. "Wilbur Langley, you're under arrest for the making and distribution of methamphetamines."

The men ran. Lexie fired a series of shots to Wilbur's left, forcing him right, as she circled toward him. Toby disappeared into the woods. Wilbur sought cover in a cluster of trees.

A big Indian *bird* flew from his perch and knocked Wilbur to the ground. Wilbur yipped like a wounded pup. Breath escaped from his body with one heavy gasp. Wilbur's long, gray hair camouflaged his face as Tye pulled him up by his shirtfront.

"Wilbur, glad we finally caught up with you."

"Your fool brother nearly broke all my bones. I ain't a big horse like him."

"Could've been worse," Tye retorted. "If I hadn't fallen on you, I would've gotten badly hurt. Unfortunately, you're so boney I may have a puncture wound."

"Let's go," Lexie ordered. "There's a jail waiting for you."

"You don't want to lock up a man who can solve that murder, does you?"

"What murder is that?" Tye said nonchalantly.

"That town woman I found dead in these woods."

"If you know something about a murder, Wilbur, you better speak fast. I'll charge you for withholding evidence, child neglect, and the multiple drug charges you've built up over the years. If you don't live past a hundred, you'll never get out of jail," Lexie warned.

"Maybe I can help, but sometimes my memory fails me when I ain't properly rewarded." Wilbur squeezed his stubby chin.

"What kind of reward do you deserve?" Tye asked gruffly.

"The sort that lets a man loose in the woods for good behavior."

"It's not happening." Lexie shrugged, "With your poor memory, you might make-up something."

"My memory is comin' back."

Tye shook his head. "Congratulations, Sis. It's your lucky day. The criminal regained his memory to save his ass."

Wilbur's lips formed into a sneaky grin. "For instance, where you found her body ain't really where she died."

"That so?" Tye responded.

"One of my kin moved the body 'cause it was too close to his work. He don't want no intruders on his property."

"I'm interested," Lexie replied. "Where's this place?"

"Oh, I can't say. This guy's a mean one, likely shoot me in the head if I messed up his operation."

Lexie placed hands on hips. "So far, Wilbur, you haven't earned a get-out-of-jail free card."

"I'm gettin' there."

"It's a slow trip," Tye quipped.

"I found something under the body."

Lexie queried, "What's that?"

"Can't say. That's the part keeps goin' in and out of my brain."

"The next time it enters your head, tell me quick," Lexie suggested. "Who knows? I might help you with the sad predicament you're in."

"I'll scratch your back, if you'll scratch mine," Wilbur winked.

"Considering your memory problem," Lexie sniped, "there's no back scratching today,"

"You'll change your mind, Sheriff Girlie."

Lexie grabbed Wilbur's arm and pulled him toward the car. She pushed him in and handcuffed him to a bar in the back seat.

"I'll see you back at the office," Tye called as he walked toward his vehicle.

Wilbur was silent on the trip to jail. Occasionally, a groan from the backseat revealed the aftermath of having a two hundred pound *bird* fall on him. His odor enveloped every crevice in the car.

Lexie rolled down the window. The warm wind brushed against her face. She felt the tears build in her eyes. A few escaped, and she smoothed them into her face. Her passenger didn't know it, but she'd make a deal with the devil to catch Abbey's killer.

Chapter Seventeen

The Diffee newspaper reporter, Adam Cox, was waiting when she arrived at the office. His long, skinny fingers reached to help her out of the car. She ignored his assistance. *Apparently, Adam hasn't grasped the concept of personal space.* She squeezed herself between him and the door.

"Sheriff Wolfe," Adam informed, "I'm writing a story about Wilbur's capture." He stood eighteen inches from Lexie and towered six to eight inches above her head. She backed away, leaving a couple of yards between them.

"Sorry, no exciting news here." Lexie rubbed her aching temple.

Adam persisted, "Wilbur has eluded arrest in this county for years. It's big news that you caught him. How'd you do it?"

"Got lucky, Tye and I captured him in the woods when we were investigating Abbey's death."

"Do you have an update on Abbey's killer?"

"The investigation is continuing."

"Do you have a suspect?" Adam probed while moving half the distance Lexie had maneuvered between them.

"Not at this time." The words reminded her of interview instructions from her cop courses.

Adam edged closer, "How soon before you make an arrest?"

She wondered if they had taught him that move in high

school journalism. "Goodbye, Adam."

Lexie unlocked Wilbur from the back seat and escorted him into the office.

Delia sat at the three-legged table while she compiled information from Abbey's murder. She glanced up when the two entered the room—then quickly returned to work.

Clay sat at his desk. His shoulders slumped and his chin rested on his chest. His bloodshot eyes followed Wilbur and Lexie into the room.

"Who told Adam about Wilbur's capture?" Lexie's lips tightened.

After a long pause, Clay confessed. " I did, we needed good news to build trust in the sheriff's office. People think we're incompetent since Abbey's murder."

Lexie wearily shook her head. "Citizens cross the street when they see me coming. Anyway, don't ever phone the newspaper without clearing it with me."

Clay nodded.

"Another thing, go home and sleep off your drunk." Lexie hoped the contempt in her voice stung through his alcoholic haze.

"Yes, boss." Clay leveraged himself out of the chair, then stumbled toward the door.

"Ain't you goin' to speak?" Wilbur challenged as he faced the back of Delia's head.

Her eyes didn't stray from the paperwork. "Hadn't planned on it."

"Too good for me, hey?" Wilbur's smoke and weather exposed face tightened leaving squinting eyes in a bed of lines and wrinkles.

Delia swerved her chair to face him. "Yes, I am. About anyone is too good for a drug selling fool."

"You didn't have a sharp tongue when you was a cute, little gal in school. As I recall, you were sweet on me then."

"With age comes wisdom. Thank God!" Delia resumed her work, her conversation with Wilbur obviously finished.

Lexie held the cell door open, "Get in your new home."

"Well, thanks! I've been needin' a rest."

"I'm thinking you're going to have a long one. However, most of it won't be here. After court tomorrow, we'll transport you to county jail."

"You speak up if you change your mind about me helpin' you find that murderer, Sheriff Girlie."

"If you decide to assist me in hopes of a reduced sentence, you do the same," Lexie countered.

"No can do, Sheriff Girlie. It's all—or nothing."

"I choose nothing," Lexie snarled.

Wilbur's laugh exploded. "Half the people in this town want you fired. Another fourth want you lynched. You need me more than I need you."

"You have a good point, Wilbur. However, unlike you, I can leave this town within twenty-four hours and never look back. On the other hand, you're sixty-two and will spend the rest of your life in the state pen. You might want to reconsider who needs whom the most."

Delia snickered.

Wilbur clamped his lips and flopped down on the cot. Within ten minutes he snored loudly.

"That man is obnoxious," Delia muttered. "Any news on the case?"

"We can't talk about it as long as Wilbur is here. He might fake sleep to get information. His preliminary hearing is at 2 p.m. After that, we'll schedule interviews with anyone connected to the team."

"Do you want a sandwich from across the street?" Delia offered.

"Yes, thanks. I can't face the hate. Please get something for Wilbur, too."

Delia rolled her eyes, then retrieved her purse and left.

Lexie wondered what the woman thought of her. Maybe she, too, believed that Lexie caused Abbey's death. Delia was more like a mother to her than her own. The thought of her disapproval brought ever-ready tears back to the surface.

The back door slammed. Lexie sprung from her chair—ready to draw her gun.

"And well you should stand in my presence," Red's blue eyes lit with humor.

"Don't be so loud!" Lexie eased back in the chair. "Most of the town hates me. I expect to be dragged to a hanging tree at any moment. What's worse, you might have aroused the sleeping drug dealer. Trust me, he's far more likeable asleep, in spite of the snoring."

"Sorry, Sheriff, I'll be gentle and dainty the next time I enter your presence." Red sat on the edge of her desk.

"To what do I owe this visit, Mr. Anderson?"

"If you need my assistance, just ask. By the way, Tye and I saw no sign of Abbey's car when we flew over the area this morning."

"I appreciate the offer. Right now I'm on hold until after Wilbur's court appearance."

Red pulled her up. His muscled arms enclosed her, and she felt loved for a few seconds.

"I'm out of here. Got a paying customer this evening. Keep your chin up." Red left as quickly as he arrived.

Lexie went into the restroom and cried. Kindness was harder to deal with than scorn. Perhaps it was because she didn't think she deserved forgiveness. She agreed with her enemies; Abbey was killed because Lexie didn't take her seriously. Now she had to find the murderer before someone else died. She washed her face then brushed and braided her hair for the first time in two days.

"Lunch is here," Delia called from the other room.

Lexie handed Wilbur his sandwich through the cell bars. She wrote notes as she chewed.

Cecil Lansbury arrived soon after their trash was tossed in the can. He was 300 pounds of ruthlessness in the courtroom, but, in person, he was the closest thing Diffee had to a gentleman. His baby-face contradicted his sixty-three years.

"Hello, Miss Delia," he said in a reverent voice.

"Hello, Cecil. Why are you defending that scum?"

Cecil's voice was gentle and steady, "Everyone gets representation, Ms. Delia."

"I know, I know, but he doesn't deserve the best attorney in the state."

Cecil blushed. "Thank you for that, Ms. Delia."

"Cecil, the three of us can walk to the courthouse together. I'll find an office for you to consult with him privately." She unlocked the cell and handcuffed Wilbur. He'd been quiet since his nap.

"Good day, Ms. Delia."

"Same to you, Cecil"

During the walk, Lexie passed Ruben and Sam sitting at their usual spot. "Hello." Ruben nodded and Sam diverted his eyes.

Wilbur didn't miss the slight. "Cecil, Sheriff Girlie has more problems than I do."

Cecil slowed his pace. "I don't know anyone who has more problems than you do, Wilbur."

Upon arrival at the courthouse, Lexie found an empty office for the pair. She spoke briefly to Assistant District Attorney Cower.

No one spoke, or even came near, while she waited on a wooden bench outside the courtroom. Finding alone time was no longer a problem.

Cecil and Wilbur reappeared at five minutes before the hour. The three made their way down the aisle, passing rows of benches on either side. They separated when they reached the front. Lexie sat down at Cower's table.

The court clerk announced, "Judge Marcus Simpson presiding."

Judge Simpson commanded, "DA Cower, what are the charges?"

Cower read from a long list: child neglect, making and distribution of drugs, and withholding evidence in a murder investigation.

Judge Simpson directed Lansbury to state his case. "My client pleads 'not guilty' to all charges. He requests release on his own merit so he can make a living for his family."

Judge Simpson slid his glasses to the end of his nose and

looked over the top at Lansbury. "That's absolutely ridiculous, Cecil."

"I know Your Honor, but that's what Mr. Langley requested."

Cower stood, "Your Honor, it has taken three years to apprehend Langley. If he's released, he'll disappear. Justice won't be served and his drug clients will be."

Judge Simpson announced, "I set bail at one million dollars."

Wilbur exploded, "HELL! No way can I come up with that kind of money."

"Transport this man to county jail. His trial will begin two months from today."

Wilbur's ravings echoed throughout the courtroom. "It ain't fair, havin' to wait two months. You all have finagled me. You and Sheriff Girlie conspired against me— that's crooked."

Simpson pounded his gavel vehemently. "I don't conspire with anyone, Langley. I'm taking a vacation in two months, so I'll see you in four. Get this guy out of my sight."

Officers grabbed an arm on each side and maneuvered Wilbur out of the courtroom.

Wilbur's voice raged from the hall. "THANKS FOR ALL YOUR HELP, ATTORNEY ASSHOLE!"

Cecil yelled back, "YOU'RE WELCOME!"

Chapter Eighteen

The newspaper hit her front door with a bang. Lexie diverted her eyes from the ceiling, which she stared at most of the night, and crawled out of bed.

Her hair was down and stray hairs stood up in front. Pajamas that slid to her hips, and a tattered T-shirt, were her apparel of choice. Her stomach growled and she realized that she hadn't eaten since lunch yesterday. Food wasn't appealing, so she retrieved the paper.

The headline was three inches high:

ABBEY KING BURIAL TODAY

Adam wrote Abbey's history including a list of her family members. At the end he quoted Lexie's statement about the investigation continuing. About mid-page was a one-inch headline that read:

NOTORIOUS DRUG DEALER
APPREHENDED BY SHERIFF

Adam did his homework on Wilbur. He summarized all previous news stories about Wilbur, as well as covered the court proceedings from the day before.

Lexie opened the closet door. She wasn't sure what to wear. The black dress was appropriate, but it made her feel feminine and vulnerable. Pulling her uniform off the hanger, she decided that she'd hide behind her sheriff persona. *Too bad I don't have armor.*

She ironed the blue slacks and shirt. After shining the badge, she pinned it on the shirt. Today, she'd pretend strength and power. Tonight, she'd allow herself to fall apart—alone.

Lexie arrived at the office a little before eight. Tye, Delia, and Clay were already at their desks.

"Delia, stay here and answer the phone," Lexie said apologetically. "I'll take your place as soon as the funeral is over. That way you can go to the cemetery and family home."

"Yes," Delia slumped against the file cabinet.

Lexie continued, "Tye, record everyone at the funeral who went to high school with you. There's apparently a tie between that class and these murders."

"Will do."

"Clay, I'm glad you didn't wear your uniform because I want you to blend in. Listen for speculations about why someone murdered Abbey."

"I didn't wear my uniform because I'm not on duty during the day. Now I have to spy on mourners?"

"Exactly, you're one of us whether it embarrasses you or not. People won't get near me, much less confide. I'll observe from the baptistery loft."

"Sounds like a good plan, Sis."

"Tye and I will be back here at 2 p.m. to interview Jamie, Beth, Loretta, and hopefully, Mariah. You two are off until tomorrow." Lexie knew that she sounded like a drill sergeant.

She drove to the funeral alone. A group of four men stared as she exited the cruiser.

One of them hollered as she walked toward the church. "What the hell are you doing here?"

She didn't respond. Soon she was within four yards of them.

"You've got some nerve coming here after what you

caused," bullied an obese man."

Lexie kept moving. Behind her a familiar voice responded to her tormenters.

"Abbey wouldn't want a scene at her funeral, or your cruelty."

The first heckler shrugged his shoulders and walked faster toward the church. The others followed.

Lexie stopped so Red could catch up.

"Got some mean people at this funeral. I'm thinking you need a body guard." A smile formed on Red's worried face.

"Maybe I should nominate you for the good Samaritan award."

"Probably so," he agreed. "However, I'll desert you soon to sit at the front. Gary asked me to serve as a pallbearer."

"He'll fire you if he sees you with me."

The pair separated at the back door. Lexie went behind the church stage and climbed to the platform behind the baptistery. Above the congregation, she could observe without being seen.

The only person Clay watched was a sexy woman. Tye searched faces as people filed into the church. Lexie wasn't sure what she was looking for—someone who cried too much, or too little? Anything that resembled a clue was appreciated.

The pews filled. People stood at the back of the church and overflowed into the balcony. *Where will the murderer sit? Probably in the balcony: he can observe without being near the family.* Of course, in this case, the theory didn't apply since there was such a crowd.

Jamie was the first person Lexie recognized as she visually scanned the balcony area. She wore a large-brimmed black hat, no doubt a new fashion accessory.

Lexie looked laboriously at each head searching for a wig or a toupee, but there were none. Row after row of sad faces was all that she saw. There was no hint of a murderer among them. Mariah said she'd come, but none of the faces resembled the girl from twenty years before. Lexie was irritated at this discovery. Now a trip to Washington was necessary.

Loretta's sobs saturated the air. Beth's head was glued to her husband's shoulder. He kept an arm securely around her. Lexie glanced at Jamie periodically. Her brother's lover sat like a statue. A tissue was never visible near her face.

At the end of the service, the ushers opened the casket. Abbey was dressed in pink. Her short, curly hair was pulled back from her face.

Megan and Travis cried out, "Mama, Mama!" Baby Nicky was in his Grandpa's arms. His small face was drawn up in anticipation of tears. He didn't understand what was happening. Gary leaned over the casket and kissed his wife for the last time.

The horror of the moment was second only to her father's murder. Lexie couldn't pretend toughness any longer. Tremors disrupted her body, and soft sobs escaped from her mouth. For twenty minutes, she remained in seclusion trying to regain control.

After she calmed, she went out the back door and circled wide around the parking lot. The thought of facing any of Abbey's family was unbearable.

*****

Delia met her at the office door and gave her a hug. She left without a word. *Maybe she doesn't hate me after all.*

Lexie forced her emotions to the background. She prepared questions for the three possible victims then arranged a table and chairs for the meeting.

Close to 2 p.m., Beth, Loretta, and Jamie entered together. Soon after, Tye arrived. They sat around the table stone-faced.

"Four of your former team members are dead. Two murdered, the third an apparent suicide, and the fourth a mercy killing. If someone is murdering your team, surely one of you can tell me why."

"We did nothing to provoke such hate," Beth volunteered.

"Probably some jealous fool," Loretta answered. "Everyone was envious of us back then."

"Name names, Loretta. Who was jealous?" Tye probed.

"I don't have names. I just know."

Lexie continued, "Did any of you get threatening notes?"

Each woman shook her head *no*.

Lexie ground the pen point into her wordless note pad. "Anyone kicked off your team?"

Again, they each responded with a negative headshake.

"Was there a guy or girl who was obsessive about any of you?"

Jamie finally contributed, "Ronald was fixated on Terri."

"He's in jail. He didn't kill Heather or Abbey," Tye responded. "Anyone else?"

"About every guy in the senior class wanted Heather," Beth contributed.

"And me," Loretta interjected. "However, none of them came after me with a poison needle."

Lexie's brows furrowed, "Was there an opposing team

that was particularly vicious?"

"We were the best in the state. They all wanted to beat us." Jamie rubbed her neck. "No one ever threatened me to my face."

Lexie looked at each of them in succession, purposely staring into their eyes. "I can't imagine that someone hates you enough to murder you, and you have no idea why. What happened that you're not telling me?"

"Don't call me a liar. We didn't have any secrets dirty enough to kill for." Loretta's voice lingered two octaves above normal.

"I don't think I'd forget something that might cost my life," Jamie added. "I'm really not that stupid."

Lexie ignored their protests. "What I hear you saying is there's no one outside your team who wanted to kill you. What about one of your own? What do you know about each other? About your coaches? About the junior varsity players?"

"This is ridiculous!" Jamie exploded. "You're pulling crap out of the air looking for someone to pin Abbey's murder on to cover your guilt. Enough of your game—I'm leaving. It's been a tough day."

"I'm with her," Loretta massaged her forehead. "My head hurts from all this chatter."

They pushed their chairs back and stood like a synchronized rebellion team.

Beth lagged behind the others, "Sorry, I'm no help."

"I hope your memories improve before one of you dies." Lexie growled the words as they exited the office.

"They're lying," Lexie said after the door slammed.

Tye shook his head. "You think they're covering for the

person who killed their friends? That doesn't make sense."

"It's not logical, but that's what's happening. Did you see anything suspicious at the funeral?"

"Fifteen people attended from my graduating class. None of them acted strangely. Clay told me he didn't see anything out of the ordinary. And you?"

"The only thing I saw out of character was Jamie wearing a black hat and sitting alone in the balcony. She didn't use a tissue during the ceremony." Lexie braced for his reaction.

"You are pulling things out of your ass. Don't imply that Jamie killed Abbey."

"As far as I'm concerned everyone is guilty until proven innocent; that includes your girlfriend."

Chapter Nineteen

Tye fingered the college basketball schedule. He wadded it in one hand and made a free throw toward the trashcan. Delia and Lexie went home at 7 p.m. and Clay was on patrol. He stopped at the window before retrieving his misguided shot, and tossed it on his desktop. Pole lights and closed signs confirmed that Diffee was locked down for the night.

He walked back to his desk and punched numbers into his phone. It rang several times before he heard the familiar, "Hello?"

"May I come over tonight, Jamie?"

"I guess, as long as we don't talk about your belligerent sister."

"She was doing her job," Tye defended.

"She needs an attitude adjustment."

"Is ten okay?"

Her "yes" ended the conversation.

There was plenty of time, so he drove along the curvy road to Mud Creek. With flashlight in hand, he exited the truck and illuminated the area. He wanted the breeze to send a message, a sign of who was in the woods with Abbey. There was no hint, only an overpowering sense of ineptness.

Driving back toward town, he thought about the shortness of life. Maybe he should ask Jamie to marry him. He asked her once years ago. Her answer was 'no' with a 'don't smother me' clause attached. She liked the sex but wasn't into hugs. Jamie was a tough woman—perhaps not mother material.

The door was unlocked when he arrived. He heard the shower running. Undressing quickly, he climbed into her bed. He made a mental note to berate her about leaving her door open when a murderer might drop by at any moment.

The light from the bathroom shone behind her naked body as she came toward him. Neither spoke as she crawled in beside him and kissed his neck passionately. After thirty minutes, they lay breathless and sweaty beside each other.

"I'm surprised you came over tonight, considering the drama at the sheriff's office."

"I wanted to be with you."

" Am I your tension reliever?"

"You can make me forget anything."

"I'm a powerful woman," Jamie sighed.

Tye kissed her hard on the lips.

"What was that for?"

"Softening you up before I complain. Why the hell did you leave your front door unlocked? You know someone wants to kill you."

Jamie sat up, "I don't believe that crap."

"There's no secret?"

She shrugged, "There are secrets, but none worth killing for."

"I came upon an interesting coincidence." Tye leaned against the headboard. His eyes focused on Jamie's reaction.

"What's that?"

"On the weekends of Heather's and Tina's murders, you coached ballgames out of town."

Jamie leaped out of bed as if on fire. "You come here and have sex with me then imply I'm a killer. You sonofabitch!"

Tye retrieved his jeans off the floor. "I'm stating a fact.

Don't get riled up. You might as well deal with the question now."

"You insinuate I'm a murderer and that's supposed to somehow benefit me? You must think I'm a fool."

"I don't think any such thing. It looks bad," Tye cautioned.

The bathroom door slammed, the lock clicked, and the shower came on. He got the message.

He put on his shirt and headed out the front door. He locked it on his way out.

Chapter Twenty

The sun rose thirty minutes before, but Lexie could barely discern it. Fog surrounded her car and it seemed to inhabit her head as well.

Her father's old saying, 'I could kick myself,' came to mind. She messed up when she interviewed Jamie, Loretta, and Beth together. It was a rookie error and she deserved to be kicked. She knew better than to allow them the power of numbers. Now she had to re-interview each of them again, individually.

First, she'd visit the states where the other murders occurred. Talking to investigating officers about similarities and possible slipups might get her a mode of operation.

The haze in her head cleared by the time she found Tye with his brown-stained coffee cup staring at a paper wad on his desk. He hadn't shaved and the black stubble blended in with the dark circles under his eyes. "You okay?"

"Couldn't sleep last night." He raised his cup and blew the steam.

"Lot of that going around." She rolled her chair to the other side of his desk to face him. "The murderer killed three women who lived out of state. Mariah should've been next. He could kill the first four without anyone realizing the deaths were connected. Unfortunately, Abbey discovered that they all died within a short period of time. My theory is that he killed Abbey out of sequence, because he wanted to shut her up."

Tye followed the logic, "Whoever killed Abbey was

someone who knew she was suspicious."

"Exactly. It was Mariah's turn to die, but Abbey screwed up the sequence."

Tye nodded his agreement.

Lexie pecked Gary's number into the phone. "Gary, it's Lexie. Tell me everyone Abbey told about the suspected murder plot." Lexie kept her words even and voice calm. This was her first conversation with Gary since the night Abbey disappeared. Her heart beat like a drum in her chest.

Gary answered laboriously, "Jamie, Beth, and Loretta when she met them about the deaths of the others. She tried to phone Mariah, but talked to her assistant instead. The guy was rude and didn't connect her with Mariah, so Abbey phoned Mariah's dad, Sean. What's this about?"

"We're working on the theory that Abbey was killed because she spooked the murderer. Did you tell anyone about this yourself?"

"No, I didn't."

"Did your daughter or Abbey's parents know her murder plot theory?"

"No one was told that she didn't think was in danger. Afraid people would think she was nuts."

"Thanks, Gary." Lexie paused, "We'll find the bastard who did this."

"Phone me when you learn something."

"We will," Lexie promised.

Tye reached for a pen. "Who we got?"

"Loretta, Jamie, Beth, Mariah, Sean, Mariah's assistant, and Gary to start the list."

"Probably their husbands," Tye concluded, "I can't imagine they didn't tell their spouses Abbey's concern."

"Beth's husband is Darren Flanders. Sam Wells is Loretta's husband. Our potential president is Donovan Toleson. At least we have a list of possibles." Lexie was heartened by the small achievement.

"Where from here?" Tye asked.

"You'll hold the fort down while I check out the other murder sites and investigation reports. It took some fast-talking with city council to get money approved for the trip. With any luck, I can get on a plane to D.C. this afternoon. I'll meet with Johnson, visit with Ronald again, and then interview Mariah."

She pushed in Johnson's number. "Stan, it's Lexie Wolfe. I'm on my way to Washington D.C. I have a murder case that's connected to Terri Womack's death. I want to compare cases."

"It's a waste of your time...except for seeing me," Johnson's voice was seductive.

"I'll convince you that it's not a waste of time. Also, I want to question Ronald again."

"Now, I'm curious," Johnson said. "Let's meet at the jail at 5 0'clock this afternoon. You can fill me in and then we'll see Ronald. Where are you staying?"

"I don't have a reservation. It was a quick decision to make the trip."

"I'll find you a room for the night."

"Well...thanks. What's the jail address?"

"1458 NE Hickory."

Tye's words shot out before she hung up. "Is pretty-boy Stan going to fix you up?"

"He's arranging my meeting with Ronald." Lexie ignored his innuendo. Her personal life was none of his business. "I have to get packed. My plane leaves Tulsa around noon. If anything comes up, call my cell."

He mumbled, "I can manage."

Lexie didn't know if it was the escape from Diffee, or the prospect of seeing Stan again, that brought on her sudden exhilaration.

Chapter Twenty-One

The phone buzzed incessantly. Bud stood on the porch. He took no pleasure from the daffodils blooming in the garden or the sun sending rays across the lawn. He suppressed the urge to smash his cell phone against the wood rail. Finally, a meek voice said, "Hello?"

"Beth, it's me, Bud. I heard about Abbey's death. Horrible!"

"The saddest funeral I've ever attended," Beth replied.

"I can't even imagine the pain this has caused her family. Have they found her murderer?"

"No. Delia told me that Lexie left today to obtain information from the investigators on the other murders."

"I'd like to see you," he urged. "Together we can figure out what's going on."

"I can't," Beth's voice squeaked. "I don't go anywhere without my husband, as Lexie ordered. I can ask him to come with me on Saturday if that works for you."

"I have a schedule conflict. I called to offer my condolences."

"Thank you."

"Yes," Bud replied.

Bud took a swallow of bourbon then hurled the glass. Fragments glittered from the floor, the chair, and his shoes. His face contorted with contained rage. *That sheriff bitch has to die.*

Chapter Twenty-Two

The flight was long and late. Lexie worried about arriving past Stan's appointed time. She rushed in the building only to find that he wasn't there. When he did appear, he offered no explanation or apology.

"Hi, Babe." He gave her shoulder a squeeze.

He was even better looking than Lexie remembered. The red shirt under his gray jacket was open at the neck showing a triangle of chest hair. His touch sent ripples through her body.

"What mystery have you brought for me to solve?" Stan spoke loud enough that two men seated in the multi-desk area looked up in interest.

"The mystery of an innocent man," Lexie proclaimed.

Stan's voice lowered, "Are we still pretending your hometown boy isn't a murderer?"

"I can't prove it yet, but I know he didn't do it."

"Enlighten me, sweetheart." Stan winked at one of the eavesdropping detectives.

Lexie felt redness blush her cheeks. "Where can we talk privately?"

"I can find a place for us to be alone. But remember, we're here to work, not play." Stan winked at the detective again.

Lexie followed him into a small, room empty of everything but dust, two chairs, and a card table.

She described the murders after Terri's and the apparent pattern. "I've no answer as to why, but I'll get there."

"Does make some sense," he stated.

Her tone sharpened, "Well, thanks. Occasionally, I'm logical!"

He pulled back, "Get those cat claws down, honey. I'm on your side."

Lexie stood. "Is Ronald ready for questioning?"

"I'll order the guard to put him in a visiting room."

The room smelled of disinfectant and body odor. Ronald sat on one of four chairs, his shoulders slumped. What little hair was present on his head at Terri's funeral was now gone. His face was drawn and his cheekbones protruded through pale skin.

"Ronald," Lexie greeted. She shook the hand he offered. "I have more questions. I know you're innocent, but I've got to prove it."

"Not even my son or parents think I'm innocent." He backhanded his cheek, wiping away the moisture that brimmed from his eyes.

"Neither did I until Lady Sheriff came around," Johnson admitted.

"Ronald, did Terri ever talk about having an enemy during her senior year? Someone who hated her and her team members?"

"Not that I remember. People thought Terri was too blunt. She was always making someone mad. What's this about?"

"Three more members of her team were murdered."

"Oh, my God!" Ronald stammered, "Who?"

"Heather, Abbey, and Tina are dead. I'm afraid the other four are in danger. Johnson reported that the man you passed in the hall the day that Terri died was never identified as visiting any other room. There's a chance he was the one who murdered Terri. What do you remember about him?"

"I wasn't paying any attention. I wanted to see Terri."

"Was he short? Tall?" Johnson questioned.

"Almost as tall as me. We were close to eye level when he looked away. Probably around six feet."

"You said that his toupee was falling off. Did you see hair underneath?" Lexie scooted closer to the chair's edge with each question.

"I don't remember any hair."

Johnson started another sequence of questions. "Was he fat? Thin? Muscular?"

"He wasn't fat."

"Here's my last question," Lexie's heart beat faster, "Is it possible the person was a woman disguised as a man?"

"I never thought about it. I guess so–a tall woman."

Lexie rose from her chair. "Thanks, Ronald. Don't give up hope. It may take weeks, but we'll get you out of here."

Ronald blew his nose on a crumpled tissue retrieved from his pocket. "Thank you." He blinked rapidly, as if trying to suppress tears.

Lexie followed Stan back to the group office. His straight man was nowhere in sight.

Stan chuckled, "That guy should've been a girl. He's such a cry baby."

Lexie poked his chest. "You really need to grow a heart in there."

The grin faded from Stan's face. "I bet you're tired. Here's the key to my place. I'll call you a cab and meet you there in two hours."

Thirty minutes later, a cab driver dropped her off at a

rundown hotel. After paying him, she looked for a sign to get directions to Stan's room, but none was visible. Finally, she saw an elderly man coming out a door. "Where's room 322?" she asked.

"Can't get in from the front—go to the back entrance."

"Thanks." She headed in the designated direction.

The room held a large bed in the middle, two stools under a kitchenette bar, a microwave, and a mini fridge. There was a small bottle of wine in the fridge but no food. She sat at the bar where she wrote notes and planned the encounter with Mariah.

Three hours later, Stan still hadn't returned. She pulled a phone book from the nightstand and found the Js. There were three Stan Johnsons listed. However, it was no surprise when one put *Det.* after his name. She dialed the number and a recording answered.

Exhausted, she climbed on the bed for a nap before the hunk returned.

A few minutes later, she heard a male voice through the haze in her head.

"Wake-up, sweetheart. I have wine and a naked man for your pleasure." Stan sat on the edge of the bed. He held two glasses of wine. "Get nude, darling, so I can see what I'm playing with."

Lexie rolled out of bed. "Excuse me for a minute, Naked Man. Let me get prepared for this experience."

After she sat on the stool, her cell phone rang. She recovered it from her pocket.

Red exclaimed, "He's married."

She snapped the phone shut, then splashed water on her face before returning to Stan.

"What's with all the clothes, baby? You want Detective Stan to strip and frisk you?"

"Do you even know my name? It's not baby, honey or sweetheart."

"After an hour with me, you won't remember your name either." Anger seeped into his words, "Quit talking and get in bed, honey, before I change my mind."

"No thanks, you're not half the man I thought you were."

"You witch! I'll send your friend to prison for life."

"If you do, I'll tell your wife that she's married to a man-whore."

Lexie grabbed her bag and went out the door. She heard a glass shatter behind her. Apparently, the hunk wasn't thirsty anymore.

She didn't know when the rain started, but there was a steady downpour. Standing under an eave, in the front of the hotel, she looked for business lights but there were none. A cab probably hadn't stopped at this hotel for a fare in ten years. Rain, and more rain, was all that she saw. The water puddled around her leather shoes and gradually covered the tops.

What am I going to do? Then she remembered the cell phone. Relief disappeared when the phone didn't have reception. After a few minutes, a government car sped around the corner. Lexie flattened against the rock building. She preferred drowning to asking the hunk for help.

She decided that walking was her best bet. Ten minutes after her march through the mud and rain began, a black truck slowed down as it approached. She jumped the ditch and eyed the passenger window going down.

"How about a ride before you drown?"

Lexie yelled across the ditch, "Red Anderson, what are you doing here?"

"Are you gettin' in the truck? Rain's blowing on my pretty shirt. Not to mention the fact that the rental place may charge extra for their flooded truck."

"You've got some nerve following me. I don't require a babysitter." Lexie struggled into the truck with her bag.

"I see you're doing fine on your own. Enjoy a little walk in the rain, do you?"

"I've had all I can take from smart-mouthed men for one day. Don't talk."

"I thought I was your knight in shining armor and all I get is a wet toad instead of a princess."

"This isn't a fairy tale, Red Anderson. It's a nightmare." Lexie clamped her lips, and put her wet head on top of her damp bag.

Red turned up the radio and sang with Alan Jackson. "Well, I'm a fool over you. It may take a while, but I'll prove it."

Lexie's head rose and looked straight ahead. "Where are you taking me?"

"I rented a motel room. We're almost there."

"Does it have two beds?"

"One for me, none for you. I thought you were spending the night with the hunk." Red continued, "I didn't think you'd fall for a pretty face. Men who love their mirrors are lousy in bed."

Lexie groaned, "How do you know?"

"A rumor I heard from my women friends."

Red parked the truck in front of the motel door. He walked around and took Lexie's bag. She was too tired to protest.

Inside the room, she headed for a hot shower. Afterwards, she put on her long nightgown. When she came out of the bathroom, Red was gone. A blanket covered the recliner, she snuggled into its warmth.

Thirty minutes later, Red returned with hamburgers and fries. After eating, she began round two of indignation.

"You have some nerve. I don't require a protector."

He reclined against two bed pillows while he looked at a sports magazine. His eyes didn't leave the page. "I know that."

"Then what the hell are you doing here?" Lexie gave him the evil eye.

"Worried about you." He avoided eye contact.

"I can take care of myself better than most men."

"I know," he turned a page.

"Did Tye put you up to this? I'll fire him."

"He didn't."

"You're lying."

Red sat up and looked into her eyes. "No, I'm not. He told me not to come. He said you'd have a fit, and you've proved him correct."

"So, why did you come?"

"I love you." Red resumed his reclining position on the bed, magazine in hand.

"You don't either love me. Quit messing with my brain."

"Pardon me, I was sure I loved you. Apparently, I should ask you how I feel rather than rely on myself."

"Be quiet and go to sleep," Lexie snapped. Pulling the blanket over her head, she shut out Red and the rest of the world.

Chapter Twenty-Three

Lexie woke to the smell of bacon.

"Here's your breakfast, Sheriff. We'll have to manage with Styrofoam instead of fine china."

"I can this once."

Red pushed an old desk between the recliner and the bed so they'd have a place to eat.

"This sure tastes good. Thanks."

"What's our plan today?"

"There's no 'our' plan, Mr. Anderson. My job is to question Mariah."

"What time are you scheduled?"

"Around 10 o'clock. My Kansas flight to investigate Tina's death leaves at two."

"I'll fly you to Kansas if you want to avoid the airport rigmarole," Red offered.

"You better fly home before I strangle you." A smile followed her words.

"You sure are a difficult woman to assist. I'll even give you a free ride to Mariah's place."

"Okay, okay, I give up. I'll take both your offers."

After finishing breakfast, they stuffed their bags and headed out the door. Much to Lexie's relief, nothing was said about the love thing from the night before. Hopefully, they'd pretend it never happened.

They got lost three times before Red finally pulled in front of Mariah's security gate.

"I'll wait down the block. Call when you're finished."

This isn't a house; it's a mansion. The place reminded Lexie of old, southern plantation homes she'd seen in photos. Huge pillars held up the third story balcony. The mansion was white with burgundy trim. The yard looked like a never-walked-on plush green carpet. Rose bushes of every color were strategically located to ensure a perfect balance between the east and west sides of the estate. The place looked like something from a storybook.

Lexie banged the knocker up and down gently. When no one answered after three minutes, she used muscle to make her presence known. The loud sound was out of place in the tranquil surroundings.

A tall man, who Lexie guessed was in his thirties, opened the door. His small-framed glasses were surrounded by straight, black, chin-length hair and bangs that covered his eyebrows. The Beatles look—forty years late.

He opened the door a few more inches. "Yes?"

"I'm Sheriff Lexie Wolfe. I have an appointment with Mrs. Toleson."

"Certainly," he opened the door. "This way, please."

Lexie followed him up the curved staircase to a second floor sitting room.

Mariah stood when Lexie entered the room. "Thank you, Wade." He grimaced and exited the room.

"He isn't in a good mood today," Lexie ascertained.

"Wade's always in a bad mood when the maid is off. He thinks domestic tasks are below him. He only wants to answer the phone and take care of my paperwork. He's my personal assistant."

"What's his last name?"

"Cartwright."

"Mariah, I'm sorry to bother you with this. Your life must be crazy with your husband on the short list for the presidential nomination." Lexie studied the statuesque woman. Mariah's hair was cut short and highlighted blonde. Her perfectly proportioned body looked elegant in the black, silk pantsuit she wore.

"Yes, it's a busy time, but don't apologize. If I can do anything to assist you, I want to do so. I admit, it greatly concerned me when I heard my own life may be in danger."

"Are you saying that it doesn't concern you now?"

"I can't imagine how the deaths are related." Mariah drew a deep breath. "Our team history was long ago, and I wasn't part of their clique. They accepted me during basketball season because I got the ball in the net."

"I asked Jamie, Loretta, and Beth for their thoughts on a possible team enemy. They didn't come up with anyone, or so they said. Frankly, I thought they lied."

Mariah straightened her shoulders, and put both feet flat on the floor. Her eyes diverted downward as she bit her bottom lip.

Lexie didn't fill the silence. She waited for Mariah to speak her mind. It didn't happen, so Lexie continued, "I think there's a secret. Perhaps it doesn't have anything to do with the murders, but there's something—I know there is."

Mariah's eyes glanced at the door, as if looking for an escape route.

"I'm here, Mariah, hoping that you'll have the courage to tell the truth. Four women have died. Surely that negates any reason for keeping a secret," Lexie said solemnly.

"I promised. My word means something."

Lexie pressed, "The truth may save four lives, including

yours."

"It's not logical that we'd be killed for what I know."

"Please, let me help you make sense of it. It's my job."

Mariah's hands clenched, "Will you tell where you got the information?"

"Not necessary to tell." Implying something that wasn't true was okay, Lexie rationalized, if it caught a killer.

"The summer before our senior year, Loretta had an abortion. My father found the midwife. They killed the baby so she wouldn't miss her senior year. It made me sick. We all swore to keep our mouths shut." Mariah dabbed at her eyes with a silk handkerchief.

Donovan appeared at the door. "Ladies, let me escort you to the dining room. Cook said that lunch is served."

Mariah's sadness ended abruptly. "Dear, this is Sheriff Lexie Wolfe from Diffee. I told you about Abbey's death."

"Yes, of course, I remember. Sorry to meet you due to a tragedy."

He reached over and gently touched Lexie's hand. He was an elegant man with a head of white hair. She thought it was real, but wasn't certain. This man could afford the most expensive hairpiece in the world.

Lunch was luxurious and filled with gourmet food and small talk about Donovan's political future.

After Wade removed the last course, Lexie initiated her best portrayal of gushy envy, "I've never seen a house as beautiful as yours. May I have a tour?"

"Certainly," Donovan answered. "I don't imagine they have mansions like this in Diffee."

"Not even close," Lexie replied.

Mariah didn't look thrilled about her tour guide

assignment. Lexie admired everything on the first and second floors. Then they entered the third floor, which was a gigantic master suite. Mariah pointed out the original art. Lexie walked, as if in a trance, taking in the beauty of her surroundings. She opened the closet door abruptly. The light came on automatically and the twelve-by-twelve space illuminated.

Mariah rushed to the closet. "I'm embarrassed. The maid didn't straighten this closet a week ago when I asked, and it's still a mess."

"My fault," Lexie apologized. "I thought it was the bathroom. Nature called."

Mariah pointed, "The bathroom is there."

Lexie didn't doubt that Mariah wanted to slap the goofy country sheriff. Lexie flushed the stool then opened the cabinet door. A lovely bronze brush yielded a strand of hair for Lexie's collection. The running water created a sound barrier when she opened the drawer beside the sink. It held a brush with a white hair. She wrapped each hair in plastic and stuck them in her bag.

Wade was present when Lexie exited the restroom. "Ms. Toleson has prior obligations this afternoon. I am to show you out."

"Oh sure," Lexie gushed. "I was a pest but this place is fabulous."

"Tell her thanks." Lexie patted Wade's back—he stiffened. "I hope you're all right. You seem sad."

"I'm fine," he said gruffly and opened the door.

Lexie jogged toward the security gate. She held the hair from the back of Wade's shirt securely between her thumb and finger. As if by magic, the security gate opened. Red waited on the other side.

"Did you stay here the entire time?"

"I got lunch. What are you wrapping up?"

"A strand of hair. You never know when a DNA sample might come in handy."

"Did you find anything interesting?"

"Most intriguing were the two toupees and a wig lined up neatly in the Toleson closet. I'll write notes while you drive to the airport. I don't want to forget anything."

"I guess that's my shut-up cue."

"You do know how to take a hint."

Lexie expected a comeback, but all she got was Red pretending to zip his lips.

Chapter Twenty-Four

Red's small plane was left to the will of an uncompromising wind. Lexie grasped her stomach, trying to stabilize the contents so it wouldn't find its way to her lap.

"I hope you don't have a weak stomach. This is the worse wind my bird has ever flown in."

"I'm okay," she said unconvinced. "I'll close my eyes."

Red landed the airplane at a small airport in Kansas after what seemed like an eternity. Lexie phoned Sheriff Sloan. He agreed to meet her at the park where Tina died. Lexie gave Red directions as he drove the rental car.

"I'll wait here," Red offered before Lexie ordered.

A short man, probably mid-sixties, moved toward her; gray, curly hair framed his bearded face. His shirt was neatly tucked, pants pressed and creased; she had no doubt that he was former military. His movement was a modified march. He stood at attention when he stopped in front of her.

"Sloan, here."

"Sheriff Wolfe, here."

He broke into a big grin. "You weren't what I was expectin'."

"And what were you expecting, sir?"

"A big, mean, ugly man."

"Mean fits from time to time, but I can't claim the gender."

"Pleasure to meet you, Sheriff Wolfe."

"It's Lexie."

"Why are you here?"

"I believe that Tina Smith was the second of four murders

by the same man—one of which happened in my town, Diffee."

"It would certainly please me to discover a relevant clue in Tina's case. Her husband has called me twice a week since she died, asking if I've found the killer. All I can say to the poor guy is 'no.' The scum left nothin' here. I'm hopin' he did somewhere else."

"What do you have?" Lexie crossed her arms and listened intently.

"Whoever did it planned well. Musta worn gloves. We found what we thought was a gray hair, but it was synthetic. You know the kind—thousands of hairpieces and wigs made from it. No car tracks. The culprit stayed on the gravel. My team is the best there is and we didn't find anything that pointed us in the right direction. We assumed it was random meanness. Of course, that doesn't explain why she left her husband's service, and ended up in a deserted park."

"The husband looked clean?"

"Gavin was collecting souls for Jesus when she died. Can't get any cleaner than that. He said that Tina didn't say anything about knowing anyone in town."

Lexie told Sloan everything she knew about the other three cases, including her saga of watered-down evidence.

"I appreciate your insights, Sheriff Lexie. If you think of other questions, phone me."

"Will do and you do the same."

Sloan lifted a hand in farewell as Red and Lexie exited the park.

Red gave Lexie an inquiring look.

"As Sheriff Sloan said, 'nothin.'"

"This is the end of the road for me, Lexie. I have a flight

in Lawton tomorrow."

"I saw a hotel near the airport. Drop me off there."

"Where's your next stop?"

"Tomorrow morning I'll fly to Dallas to research Heather's case. I'm back home late tomorrow night."

Red drove in front of the hotel. He pulled Lexie's bag from the back seat.

"Here we go again," she protested. "I can get my own bag. Remember, I'm a gun-toting sheriff."

"You may be everyone else's sheriff, but you're my girl."

"I'm sorry I was such a bitch last night."

"You had a bad day."

He pulled her to his chest and kissed her long and firmly. Without a word, he got in the vehicle and headed toward the airport.

I haven't had a kiss like that in fifteen years. Interesting that it was the same guy delivering. Her mind wandered back to that day. Red often spent the night at their house with his best friend, Tye. That particular morning, Tye and her dad left early to fish. Her mom didn't wake until after 10 a.m.

Lexie shed her bathrobe and crawled into bed beside Red, who was sound asleep. She gently smoothed the red hair back from his forehead. Rubbing his chest she caught hairs between her fingers and made paths across his chest. Ripples of passion possessed her body. Her hand drifted to his belly.

She startled when he moved. He turned to his side and held her. His mouth pressed against hers. Their tongues touched, then he turned away. "Go away," he snarled.

Lexie remembered the hatred she felt for months. The rejection and embarrassment were too much for her teenybopper brain. As far as she knew, he never told anyone about her foiled attempt at seduction. Not counting today, it was the best kiss ever.

Chapter Twenty-Five

Lexie couldn't remember the last time she slept so soundly. The alarm rang at 6 a.m. and her body refused to move from the bed. She pressed her lips against the back of her hand trying to recreate the feeling of Red's kiss. It didn't work.

In the shower, she mentally chastised herself for giving in to sloppy emotions. "I don't have time to waste on foolishness. I've got to find this murderer," she proclaimed.

After the shower, it was rush to the airport, maneuver through security, and board the plane. Finally, she was securely fastened in her seat, ready for the takeoff.

Her mind dwelled on Loretta's alleged abortion and its connection, if any, to the murders. It was possible this was the secret. Even if it wasn't, perhaps she could bait Loretta into telling what her girlfriends were concealing. *Why now and not five, ten, fifteen years ago?*

Gazing out the window, she hoped that she'd find evidence in Dallas since Kansas was a bust. She was intrigued by the fact that District Attorney Lave Blanchard volunteered to chauffer her around the city. A stewardess interrupted her thoughts with landing instructions. The plane's tires soon hit the runway.

When she exited the plane, it was easy to spot Blanchard holding a red sheet of paper—their contact sign. She reached out her hand, "I'm Lexie Wolfe."

"Good to meet you. I'm Lave."

The muscles in his arm rippled when he reached for her

bag. His head was shaved clean. The man looked like the poster guy for masculinity.

Two stewardesses eyed him up and down, obviously appreciating the view. Lave flashed them a teeth-whitener commercial smile.

His cocky attitude immediately reminded her of Johnson. Lexie wondered who'd get the mirror if there was only one in a room they shared. She interrupted the flirting, "I'm ready if you are."

He gave his admirers another smile, "I'm good to go."

"Lave, I'm surprised that a big city DA volunteered to chauffer a small town sheriff. What's that about?"

"I like a woman who shoots from the hip. Not much of a mystery. Heather was my wife. We divorced a few months before she died. Got it in her fool head that I cheated. She left me."

"Sounds like she was insecure about your relationship."

"For sure. She started therapy sessions because she was screwed up. Psychiatrist's name is Williams. He acted like a fool at the funeral."

"How's that?" Lexie asked.

"When he saw me in the church entry, he pressed against my shoulder. Told me I had no right to attend her funeral. I would've broken him in half if I wasn't in a church." Lave's knuckles turned white from the strength of his grip on the wheel.

"Did you have a woman with you?"

"How do you know?"

"I figured a man who looked as good as you had women panting on the side hoping to be next in line."

Lave laughed and his shiny teeth made another showing.

"Well, thanks, Lexie. I got an offer from a babe, quick. I know it didn't look appropriate, but a man has his needs."

Sometimes a man needs neutered. Lexie replied, "I hear you."

"Detective Chandler told me that you think Heather was murdered."

"She's the investigating officer I phoned. Chandler determined that your wife committed suicide. I told her I doubted that decision, due to three of Heather's friends dying within a short period of time. I believe someone is killing the women who played on Heather's high school basketball team.

Lave's tone intensified, "Can you prove it?"

"Not yet, but I will."

"Girl, it's a jackpot for me if Heather was murdered."

"Why?" Lexie tried to say the word nonchalantly, which was difficult since she wanted to choke him.

"Heather had a fifty thousand dollar life insurance policy. I'll get the money if she didn't commit suicide. If murder isn't proven—that money is down the drain."

"OH!" Lexie knew she blew the nonjudgmental sheriff role with the tone of her voice but she didn't care. The guy was a class A-ASS.

DA Lave went defensive. "It sounds terrible. But you know she loved me or she wouldn't have left it to me. I can afford to buy her a nice headstone and help her old man out, if she was murdered."

"That's a good plan." Lexie regretted that solving the murders would give the jerk a payoff.

At the police station, Lave walked her to Sarah Chandler's office. "Hi there, sweet thing." He sat on the corner of her desk.

Sarah, a sturdily built woman, didn't look like she'd take any crap and probably hadn't for the last twenty years. "Get your rear off my desk," she ordered.

Lave slid off, "Crabby today?"

"You know it, hotshot. I'm cranky every day 'cause you DAs don't know how to solve cases after we catch the crooks. Don't you have any manners? Who's that with you?"

"This is Sheriff Lexie Wolfe. She's the one who'll solve Heather's case. You know, the case you screwed up."

"Get out of here, smart mouth."

As soon as the door closed behind Lave, Sarah remarked, "I didn't notice you drooling over Mr. America."

"Head's too big," Lexie replied. "You aren't under his spell either?"

"I got older and smarter. It's not good looks; it's money that I'm after." Sarah chuckled. "So what do you know Sheriff Wolfe that will turn my suicide case into a murder?"

Sarah listened intently as Lexie reviewed the cases.

"I see where you're coming from, but you're a long way from proof."

Lexie knew Sarah was right. "Was Heather checked for poison or needle marks?"

"No, she wasn't, I'm embarrassed to say. With her history, it seemed damn clear that she'd caused her own death. I interviewed her dad and psychiatrist. They verified that she was suicidal, so I closed the case. It really pissed off Lave since he didn't get the insurance money. If you're right, he'll be one happy man."

"Makes me hope I'm wrong."

"Me, too," Sarah acceded.

"If it's okay with you, I'd like to question Dr. Williams."

"I'll have the clerk call and set-up the meeting," Sarah agreed.

Five minutes later, a clerk opened the door. "Dr. Williams said he's available all afternoon."

"Let's go," Sarah stood.

"I have a request, Sarah."

"What's that?"

"No Lave."

"You're a perceptive woman, Lexie. I'll tell him to get lost."

"I just met you, but I've already bonded."

"Mutual," Sarah smiled.

DA Lave sat on the desk of a cute young clerk. "Doesn't your big ass fit in a chair?" Sarah blurted.

Lave jumped from the desk as if his rear was struck by lightning. His lips puckered, "My butt isn't big."

"You missed the point, Mr. Ego."

Lave placed a hand on his chest. "The point struck right in my heart."

"Funny boy, I'm taking Lexie off your hands. We'll interview Dr. Williams, then I'll drive her to the airport."

"I'd like to tag along," Lave coaxed.

"Get your nose out of my case."

"I'll leave it to the Dynamic Dame Duo to retrieve my money."

Lexie followed Sarah toward the door. "Thanks for the ride, Lave."

He saluted, "Anytime, honey, anytime."

Sarah received a call as soon as they took off. The drive was filled with Sarah giving the rookie directions. Lexie was fine with that. She mentally rehearsed questions for the doctor. For some reason, she wanted to impress Sarah.

*****

Sarah approached his desk, "Dr. Williams, this is Sheriff Lexie Wolfe from Oklahoma. She has an interesting theory about Heather's death."

He rose and extended his hand. He wore a long linen shirt, brown trousers, and loafers—*a classy guy.*

Lexie shook his outstretched hand. "Thank you for agreeing to see me."

"You're welcome. However, I thought the investigation into Heather's death was closed."

"I'm here because three women she knew died during the same time period, all apparent murders. If we don't find the killer soon, four more may die."

"That's disturbing." He covered his mouth then stroked his beard.

"Your assistance may substantiate my theory. Will you help Dr. Williams?"

His fingers made circular motions around his mouth. "Heather was a beautiful woman. She was caring and funny, when she wasn't overwrought with pain caused by her idiot husband."

Lexie concurred, "I met the jerk. He was on a mission to get that insurance payoff."

Williams focused on Sarah, "I couldn't stand for him to get that money. But now, if other women may die, there's someone out there worse than him."

"Did Heather commit suicide?" Lexie probed.

"Very unlikely," he confessed. "I saw her the night before. She was agitated because she neglected to remove Lave from the life insurance policy. Heather said that 'DA Lave and his whore princess,' wouldn't benefit from her death. No way would she have killed herself before making her father the beneficiary on that policy.

"Anything else that made you think it wasn't a suicide?" Lexie was surprised that Sarah hadn't said a word or asked a question since the interview started.

"She promised to go inpatient. She was ready to get well." His tongue stumbled over the words.

"Did she know how you felt about her?"

"You are an intuitive woman, Sheriff Wolfe. I told her that night. I referred her to a new psychiatrist because I loved her. She squeezed my hand before she left this office. When she died, it took my heart and part of my soul."

Sarah finally spoke, "Why didn't you tell me what you really thought?"

"I made sure her ex-husband didn't get the money. I saw it as the last thing I could do for her. That's why I substantiated the suicide theory. I never believed it was true. Once I heard the message, it solidified my belief."

"Message?" Lexie and Sarah blurted in unison.

"It came in that morning when I was with a client. I saved it to hear her voice."

Dr. Williams pushed a button on his answering machine. A cheerful voice conveyed a message, "Paul, it's Heather. I'm doing fine and getting packed. An old friend from high school is dropping by to see me this morning. I'm so excited! I'll talk to you soon."

Sarah paced, "Based on that tape, I have no doubt

Heather was murdered."

"Nor do I," Lexie agreed.

"Detective Chandler, will you charge me for withholding evidence?" Williams fingered his beard.

"It just took a while to speak up, so you didn't really withhold it." Sarah continued, "I'll take that tape, but I'll do my best to get it back to you."

Lexie concluded, "Thank you. I know it's a struggle to let go of what you knew Heather wanted, but you're helping find her murderer."

"Lave is the lesser of two evils," Chandler added.

"I know," responded the doctor.

After their goodbyes, they jogged to the car, both aware of Lexie's short timeline to catch her flight.

Sarah monitored the rush-hour traffic as she spoke, "Williams is a fine example of someone screwing up a detective's work. I felt sorry for him, but I should charge him, or at least kick him, for not telling the truth."

Lexie laughed, "I'd hold him down for you."

Sarah's aggravation lifted, "That's what I call teamwork. Forget about those work relationship seminars the brass forced me to attend. A good ass kickin' would make for a great bonding activity."

"They'd have my vote," Lexie agreed.

Sarah pulled in front of the terminal. "I'll keep in touch regarding the investigation here, and you do the same."

"Will do."

"If you ever want a job in Dallas, call me."

"Thanks, but I've got much work to do in Diffee before I consider moving on."

The women exchanged waves. Lexie quickened her pace.

Now she was at the most difficult part of her trip—getting her bearings at the Dallas Airport. After following three different pointing fingers, she reached the right gate. A voice over the loud speaker confirmed her flight: "TULSA flight 273: On Time."

It'll be good to get back home, she thought, as she maneuvered into her seat.

Chapter Twenty-Six

Bud held the fine leather suitcase with care. He was purposely running late for flight 273 to Tulsa.

"I'm so sorry," He apologized to the half dozen people in front of him in line. "My meeting ran over and I fear I'll miss my flight. May I go in front of you?"

Each of the six nodded or motioned for the distinguished looking man to move ahead. His appreciative smile negotiated him through his dilemma.

The woman, at the counter, checked his identification and put his bag on the conveyer. "You better run," she advised.

Bud made long strides toward the escalator until he was out of sight of the check-in desk. He exited at the first door and hailed a cab to transport him to the other Dallas airport.

Chapter Twenty-Seven

Lexie visually scanned the inside of the plane. There wasn't a single empty seat. A college basketball team occupied many of the spaces. There was a group of tanned ladies who connected from Hawaii to Dallas to Tulsa. A baby cried at the back of the plane. A toddler escaped from his daddy and ventured a few rows. Everyone in his path received a friendly grin. Lexie usually sat in the escape row, but basketball players already inhabited those seats. Her only choice was to sit near the rear of the plane.

Two young women talked about their father's heart attack, and their hope he'd live until they saw him one more time.

Her seatmates introduced themselves, "We're Larry and Connie Matthews."

"I'm Lexie Wolfe."

"On vacation, Lexie?" Connie asked.

"No, had work in Dallas. Were you two on vacation?"

"If you consider spending four days with thirty-two of Connie's relatives a vacation, then I guess we did have one." Connie reached over and playfully pinched Larry's cheek.

"Twenty-four of them are on this flight," Connie added.

"I won't pick a fight with you two. I can't handle twenty-six to one."

"Let me warn you that flying scares my wife to death. Ignore her, if she screams like a fool. Connie took a sedative before she came on board. I pray she'll fall asleep instead of driving me nuts."

"It's actually safer than driving," Lexie comforted.

Chapter Twenty-Eight

Irritation brought beads of sweat to Leo's forehead as he pulled luggage off the bag belt. He had to load it and deliver it to flight 273. The airport was unusually busy during his shift. He didn't dare risk looking in any of the luggage to see what treasures he could sneak into his trash bag. Usually, he managed to get his hands on at least a hundred dollars worth of jewelry, tech stuff, cameras, or even cash during his shift but, today, his bag was flat.

It wasn't so much the money as his pride. During two months of employment as an airport ramp agent, he stole something every shift. Flight 273 was the last flight of his day. Time was running out to keep his record intact.

"Get a move on, Leo," his boss hollered, "that Tulsa flight leaves in fifteen minutes. I'll write you up if that baggage misses the plane!"

Leo's small frame tensed and a flash of anger turned his face crimson. He threw the rest of the bags on the cart.

"Grab that last one," the boss ordered, then walked toward the break-room.

Leo's eyes scanned the area. The fine leather suitcase disappeared into his trash bag. He dumped the trashcan contents over it. He left his treasure and rushed the other luggage to the plane.

Back at the baggage area, Leo punched the time clock and grabbed his trash bag along with two other full bags of trash. His old car was parked, as usual, near the dumpster. He heaved the two heavy bags into the dumpster, then pushed his treasure bag into the trunk.

"I'm the master," Leo muttered, "the best of the best." He spent his time behind the wheel imagining what the leather bag held. A pile of money was a nice thought, or perhaps it was full of jewelry: diamonds, rubies, emeralds, or pearls. It looked like his worse day might turn into his best day ever.

Leo made a sharp right off the highway onto the mile long dirt road that led to his house. His excitement built as he pulled the bag from the trunk.

He pushed the dirty dishes to the side of his kitchen table, and ceremoniously put the bag in the middle. Using a screwdriver, he disengaged the lock then pulled the zipper. His eyes widened. A long piercing scream escaped from his throat. He ran toward the door. Too late! The explosion sent him, his house, and the fine leather bag skyward.

Chapter Twenty-Nine

"Goodbye," Lexie said. "Nice meeting you."

"Same to you," Larry replied.

"I'm glad we didn't crash." The tenseness in Connie's face subsided.

Larry's face crunched in disgust. "This is getting old. A plane hasn't crashed with you on it yet. Don't be such a damn drama queen."

Connie hugged Lexie. "I'll be braver next time."

Lexie nodded with a comforting smile.

Finally, the front passengers moved forward. Eventually, Lexie slept soundly in her own bed.

Chapter Thirty

Lexie arrived at her office promptly at 7 a.m. eager to discuss her findings with Tye. She looked through her phone messages. One each day was from Wilbur who wanted to negotiate a deal. Apparently, jail time softened his position. There were several calls from Abbey's family members yelling for an arrest.

As she hoped, Tye arrived before Delia. "Little sister, are you adventured out?"

"Absolutely."

Tye sat on the edge of her desk. "What did you learn?"

"Nothing to help with Abbey's case. Johnson did sway from his belief that Ronald murdered Terri, but he kept him locked up. No way was Heather's death a suicide. Detective Chandler reopened the case and will have the body exhumed."

"Why are you so sure about Heather?"

"Because there was a cheerful message on her psychiatrist's answering machine. It said she was excited because an old friend from high school was coming to visit. That was the morning she died."

"I'll be damned."

"Pull out your list," Lexie directed. "By the way, Ronald said the man in the hall outside Terri's hospital room was around six feet. I assume he passed the murderer. The sheriff in Kansas reported a gray synthetic hair on Tina's body.

"Since she said 'high school friend' that means we can rule out Beth, Tina, Mariah, and Heather's husbands," Tye reasoned.

Lexie continued, "That leaves Jamie, Beth, Mariah, Gary, Loretta, and her husband Sam. They all knew Abbey's suspicions and went to high school with Heather. I can't imagine she'd refer to Sean as a 'high school friend,' but we'll leave him on the list."

"Beth is too short, so she's off the A list," Tye added.

"Perhaps a coincidence, but I saw two gray toupees and one wig in the Toleson closet. Her husband's hair looked natural, but I'm not positive. Rich people can afford hairpieces that look real."

"Of course, any husband may help his wife do the killing if he thinks it's important enough," Tye noted.

"I know, but I want a short list to concentrate on at this point. There are too many possibilities if we look at everyone who went to high school then."

Lexie grabbed the phone on the first ring, "Sheriff's office."

"This is Chandler."

"Sarah, hello. Has something happened since I left?"

Her voice was all business. "Have you seen the news today?"

"No, I was in a hurry to get to work."

"Listen to the news then phone me back," Chandler ordered.

"What's going on?" Tye questioned as she moved to the radio located on the corner shelf.

"Sarah said, 'listen to the news.' Didn't say why."

Lexie found the broadcast then sat back and waited. It didn't take long before an official sounding voice gave the report.

"A rural area outside of Dallas was rocked by a bomb yesterday evening. A baggage man from the Dallas airport was killed in the explosion. No other deaths were reported. The baggage man was under suspicion a month ago when a fellow employee accused him of stealing from a suitcase. Due to a lack of evidence, he was not charged or fired."

The reporter played a previously taped interview with Detective Sarah Chandler.

"Do you think this was a terrorist act, Detective?"

"No."

"What's your theory?"

"I'm working on the assumption that Leo Dunham stole the bag hoping there was something expensive inside. I imagine it was quite a shock when he found a bomb."

The reporter was direct, "You believe the bomb was meant to blow up a plane?"

"Yes," Sarah replied confidently.

"What flight was it supposed to end up on?"

"Flight 273 to Tulsa was the last flight Dunham loaded baggage on. Looks like that was the intended target."

The reporter persisted, "Why are you so sure it wasn't a terrorist?"

"There's no way to be certain." Sarah continued, "I do know there was a murder investigator on that flight. At this point in time, I believe she's getting close to the killer, and he tried to get rid of her permanently."

"Whose murder?" Excitement was evident in the reporter's voice.

"Not talking about that now," Sarah said firmly. "This is a theory with some back-up proof, but time will tell."

"Are you saying a lowlife thief saved the lives of over a

hundred passengers because he stole a bomb?" The reporter sounded elated.

"That's what I think, but as I said, time will tell."

Lexie turned off the radio. Her arms and legs moved in short stiff jerks. She opened her mouth to suck in air. Crossing her arms tightly in front of her chest, she gripped her shoulders in an attempt to control her emotions. The faces of Connie, Larry, and the toddler flashed in her mind. She almost got them killed.

"MY GOD, that was your flight! The sonofabitch tried to blow you up!" Tye's desk rattled as he pounded the surface with both hands.

Lexie pressed in Sarah's number. "I heard," her voice trembled.

"He's obviously alarmed," Sarah cautioned, "or he wouldn't have risk getting caught. Stay on constant vigil."

Lexie's hand squeezed the receiver, "I will."

"As I find out more, I'll get the info to you. This case must get solved as soon as possible. Be careful," Sarah warned.

"Yes," Lexie agreed.

Tye squeezed her arm. "I never thought I'd say these words, but thank God for a thief."

Lexie felt her body gradually return to near normal with the exception of the relentless pain in her head. Maybe changing the subject would alleviate the pressure.

"D...D...Did you get an invitation to your high school reunion?" she stuttered.

"It arrived yesterday. How'd you know?"

"Mariah told me she received one. I don't know about this. It's like sending an engraved invitation to a murderer."

"Beth sent out the invitations," Tye informed. "I asked her if she thought it was the thing to do under the circumstances. She's hell-bent on finishing Abbey's gymnasium project."

"We'll have all the players here at the same time. I don't know how we'll keep Jamie, Beth, Mariah, and Loretta safe."

"And you," Tye added. "Did Mariah reveal why someone was killing the players?"

"She wasn't part of their clique. She didn't think that anyone who wanted to kill them would necessarily want her dead."

"Probably true, she was different from the others—more aloof, snobbish acting."

"Mariah said that Loretta had an abortion the summer before senior year. It's possible the abortion is the secret."

"That would've caused ferocious Diffee gossip if it went public." Tye's forehead furrowed.

The door squeaked open to reveal Delia in her red and yellow flowered dress. "Welcome back, Lexie. Did Tye tell you about my doctor's appointment?"

"He did not."

"I'm guilty as charged," he admitted.

"That's a man for you. Why I never found me one."

"The way Cecil looks at you, I think he's yours for the asking," Lexie smiled.

"Old Cecil's better than most, but still too much work."

"I won't argue that point."

"Did you find evidence to solve the murders?"

"Got information—no real help. You'll read about it when you process my notes." Lexie headed for the door. "I'll pay Wilbur a visit, maybe he's ready to talk.

"He's sure anxious," Delia pondered. "He doesn't enjoy his new home."

Chapter Thirty-One

"Wilbur Langley," Lexie exclaimed when the guard escorted her into the visiting area. "What do you want?"

"This place is driving me nuts. I'm a woodsman. I can't live in a cage. This place is full of crazy men!"

"Probably loony because you fried their brains with drugs."

Wilbur's tone intensified, "I'm ready to deal."

"Are you now? Here's my problem. I don't know what I'm receiving from your so-called deal."

"Take a chance, Sheriff Girlie."

"I'd look a fool if I helped a criminal and got nothing in return."

"People might not hate you quite so much if you caught the murderer." His small eyeballs fixed on her.

"It rained, so whatever you found is useless." Lexie started toward the door.

His voice croaked desperation, "No, don't leave. You gotta help me."

Lexie stomped the floor, "No, I don't."

"The object was under her body; the rain didn't hurt it. You won't find it without me."

Lexie summoned the guard, "Get the jailer."

"This is a bad idea, Sheriff," Jailer Harris protested. "The judge should be called."

"I'm borrowing him, Harris. Remember, I captured him. He claims there's a clue to Abbey's murder hidden in the woods. I must find out if he has anything."

"Okay," Harris growled, "but this is all on you if there's a problem. Sign him out."

Harris handcuffed Wilbur and walked him to the patrol car. Lexie locked him to the bar across the back seat. She viewed Harris' stiff stance as she turned the car out of the lot.

Wilbur breathed in deeply when they reached their destination. "Good to see the woods again."

Lexie pulled his arms behind him, and cuffed the link from the bar onto his free hand. "Okay, Wilbur, lead the way. Remember, my gun is right behind you."

He walked curves around the trees for at least twenty minutes. "It's here," he hollered, pointing his chin toward an old saddlebag flung high in a tree.

She faced Wilbur toward a tree, then opened the ring from his right wrist in order to pull his arm in a circle around the tree to his left wrist. He ripped his arm from her grasp and swirled around. The metal ring slapped against her neck as he pushed her down. He ran.

Struggling to her feet, she fired a shot to his right and stumbled. She recovered, but a few yards later, he vanished in the underbrush. She stopped and listened for running steps, or the clank of the unsecured link, but there was nothing. She wandered aimlessly; sound gave her no direction.

I've got to turn back or I'll lose the bag location.
Tracking back to the site, her mind dwelled on her foolishness. The pouch required checking even though it was probably empty. The bark bit her skin as she climbed the tree. Stretching her arm at full length, she secured the bag in one hand and started the treacherous downward trip. Safe on the ground, she bent from the waist to calm her rapid heartbeat. She reached inside the pouch and pulled out a

small plastic bag with a hard object inside. Her momentary exhilaration depleted to zero. It was a long skinny tube of lip gloss. *What a joke! All the Diffee residents will say, 'Just like a woman—trading a drug dealer for lip gloss.' A million laughs for the rednecks.*

*****

She stopped by Gary King's house on the way home. Megan answered the door. "Dad's still at work."

"You're more likely to know than your Dad," Lexie held the plastic bag open, "did your Mom wear lip gloss like this?"

"She used those fat tubes of lipstick."

"Thanks," Lexie said.

Megan shut the door.

Lexie wondered at the girl's lack of curiosity. Based on Megan's somberness, it appeared that depression had set in as a result of her mom's death. *One more thing to feel guilty about.*

Back at her office, Lexie immediately processed the tube for prints and there, as big as life, was a thumb and a fingerprint. Abbey's fingerprints and DNA were taken before her burial. She pulled copies of Abbey's prints from the folder. An expert at fingerprints she was not, but these clearly did not match.

Allowing herself hope was ridiculous considering Wilbur's history. Even if he told the truth, it didn't mean that the killer dropped the tube in the woods. A horrible thought crossed her mind. *Were they Wilbur's prints?* She pulled his folder out—more fearful of the prints matching Wilbur's than facing Harris and the judge. Her breath came out in one long huff when she determined the prints weren't his either. Now it was time to face Harris.

"Where is he?" Harris' voice resonated through the third floor jail as soon as her foot hit the top step.

"He escaped when I was handcuffing him to a tree."

"Why the hell Diffee elected a woman sheriff, I'll never figure out!" Harris shouted his final words: "This is your ass—not mine!"

Lexie's voice was smooth as vinyl. "I'll take the responsibility."

A clerk peered around the corner. Lexie assumed the woman wanted visual confirmation of the fighters before she started the gossip chain. Workers stared as she walked down the hall and descended the steps. Prisoners cheered as she exited the building. One of their own escaped, thanks to Lexie.

As she trudged down the sidewalk, someone patterned her steady footsteps from behind.

"Sheriff Wolfe." Adam's long strides easily caught up with her. "I heard the jailer yelling at you. What's going on?"

Lexie didn't slow, but the long-legged reporter had no difficulty equaling her pace. "Wilbur Langley escaped when he was in my custody."

"Why did you take him out?"

"He hid an object that he found at the scene of Abbey's murder. I took him to recover it. I was re-handcuffing him when he broke away."

"That's what the mark on your neck is from?"

"Yes."

"Did you recover the object?"

Lexie slowed, "Yes, I did."

He shortened his stride, "What was it?"

"Can't report on that yet, but I'll keep you informed." Her steps quickened.

"You never keep me informed." Adam let his professional demeanor and his gait lapse.

"Goodbye, Adam." She gave a half-hearted wave and hoped the kid wouldn't come after her.

Chapter Thirty-Two

Lexie startled from sleep when the newspaper hit her front door with more vengeance than usual. Curious to know if Adam vented anger through his story, she retrieved the paper and sat at the kitchen table drinking coffee. FOUND AND LOST was the headline. It started with, 'Sheriff Lexie Wolfe nabbed a notorious drug dealer days ago only to lose him yesterday when he escaped into the woods.'

The paragraphs continued with Lexie's brief comments from the day before and a recap of Abbey's murder. The article ended with 'the murderer is still at large.' Adam was fair. He even mentioned her neck injury, which verified that she didn't give up easily. Maybe she 'd give the guy a break.

It was a tough day ahead. Delia scheduled interview times with Beth, Jamie, and Loretta. Lexie hoped they'd give their fingerprints and DNA without subpoenas. Mariah was the easiest one to check since she was overseas when her dad was on military duty. It was a pain to think about a trip back to Washington to get prints, hopefully they'd be from Interpol. She sure didn't want to ask the hunk for help. She berated herself to stop thinking and take a shower.

Within an hour, she stood beside her desk watching Beth enter. Tye pulled the old table out for them to sit around. Delia fidgeted with the pen that was about to record hours of information.

Lexie rubbed her hands together. "Thanks for coming, Beth."

The legs scraped when Beth pulled out the chair. She

wore a long sleeved, high-collared navy dress. Her hair was swept into a bun. Her straight back and set mouth didn't soften as Lexie began the interview.

"I was shocked that you're leading the fund raiser."

"It's for Abbey. She wanted to honor Terri and I wouldn't feel right if I didn't try."

"Considering that you invited someone who wants you dead, I think you made a mistake," Lexie drilled the words toward Beth.

"What makes you think I invited the killer?"

"Heather left a phone message on the morning she died. She said an old friend from high school was coming to visit. Now she's dead."

Tye took the good cop role. "Beth isn't the type that anyone would murder."

"The murderer poisoned a woman almost dead from cancer," Lexie responded. "He doesn't have limits on who he's willing to kill."

"I'm sorry, I'm sorry. I shouldn't have sent out the invitations, but I wanted to honor my dead friends."

"Honor Abbey by helping us find her killer. What did you see, or hear, or know, in high school that makes it necessary to kill you?" Lexie questioned.

"Nothing," Beth whimpered.

Anger seeped into Lexie's words. "There's something, or your friends wouldn't be dead."

"It won't happen to me," Beth murmured, "everyone knows that I don't divulge secrets."

"Secrets?" Tye repeated.

Her neck changed from pale to blotchy red. "Anyone's secret about anything." Beth struggled from the chair.

"Darren's waiting in the car. I'm making him late for work—again."

"Maybe if someone, LIKE YOU, told us why someone is murdering team members, then your life could return to normal," Lexie challenged as she peered into Beth's eyes.

Beth's gaze dropped to the floor, and her hands grasped her head.

"Give me a DNA sample and your fingerprints," Lexie prodded.

"You think I killed my friends?"

"No, we don't," Tye answered, "but we can't show any favoritism."

"Get it done." No effort was made to dry the tears that accumulated on her cheeks.

Lexie put on gloves and swiped the DNA swab. After Tye finished with the fingerprinting, Beth went out the door.

"She forgot to say goodbye!" Lexie scoffed.

"You were tough," Tye confronted. "Why so sarcastic?"

"Because she knows something. She probably thinks it's unrelated to the deaths, but if it's related, she's aiding a murderer."

Delia spoke softly, "She seemed frightened."

"Should be more scared than she is." Lexie popped an aspirin then took a long drink of water.

Jamie's strides were long and her face set in a scowl as she crossed the office. She wore a gray jogging suit with a black T-shirt, appropriate attire for someone who wanted to run as far as possible from Lexie's belligerent questions.

Lexie asked Jamie for samples first, rather than last, since she expected more anger as the questioning advanced. "As part of our investigation, we're asking everyone involved for a DNA sample and fingerprints."

"Since I'm a suspect, I bet you'd like mine without a fuss."

Lexie countered, "It's easier if you volunteer, but the judge can get an order over here within thirty minutes if you don't cooperate."

"Take anything you want then start your interrogation. Isn't that how it works, Tye?"

"I don't think you're a murderer, but that's my opinion and the law requires proof."

Jamie's nostrils puffed slightly. "Can't we get on with this? I've got things to do."

"Earlier today, Beth mentioned a secret, and I require more information." Lexie returned Jamie's stare.

"Then ask her."

"Beth cried. I figure a tough woman like you can share without the emotion."

"I have nothing to confide. I'm not aware of Beth's secrets. Obviously, she has one she doesn't want shared with you."

Lexie pursued, "And you, Jamie, what secrets do you know that resulted in Abbey, Terri, Heather, and Tina dying?"

Jamie's body stiffened, "As I've said before, we did nothing that deserved vengeance."

"This guy is psycho," Delia interjected, then glanced at Lexie. "Sorry."

"Delia's right. This person isn't normal. Something irrelevant to us is a personal affront to him."

Jamie wearily shook her head. "Let me repeat, I don't have anything to tell."

It was time for Lexie's shock tactic. "Do you think this is related to the abortion Loretta had during your senior year?"

The sternness in Jamie's face turned to mush.

Lexie continued, "The abortion, Jamie. The one your team covered up. Was the father angry?"

"I heard that he never knew."

Lexie probed, "You aren't positive. Maybe he kept quiet. Now, twenty years later, he's mad because you girls killed his baby."

"It's not him."

"How do you know?"

"Loretta told me that he died in a motorcycle wreck."

Lexie accused, "His family lost a grandchild because of your team."

Jamie moistened her lips. "They didn't know about the baby. His dad was a preacher and would've condemned them to hell fire for having premarital sex."

"Did anyone want Loretta to keep the baby? Did her parents know?"

"They didn't know. At the time, none of us thought of the baby as a real person, just a disruption in our basketball season."

"Anyone try to talk Loretta out of the abortion?" Tye asked.

"Abbey and Beth tried, but Loretta had made up her mind. No way was she missing her senior year."

"That's all for now." Lexie stood abruptly.

The room was silent as Jamie exited with short strides and slouched shoulders. Lexie closed the door behind her. "This is getting interesting."

Delia's head moved from side-to-side. "Hard to believe

the story didn't get out in our nosey town."

Tye stretched. "Apparently, people can keep their mouths shut."

"Unfortunately, now is a lousy time to keep secrets," Lexie added.

Chapter Thirty-Three

Loretta, as expected, arrived late. Even though Lexie wasn't surprised, she was irritated at the disrespect it indicated.

"Don't blow up," Tye cautioned, "if she clams up, you'll get nothing."

"I have a feeling Loretta will say plenty." Lexie couldn't suppress a smile.

"I'm here. I'm here." Loretta invaded the room with two large shopping bags. Her hair was disheveled and her dark roots in need of color. Even her nails weren't the usual chip free perfection. "Don't look at me like I'm a criminal. I'm only five minutes late."

"Actually, you're twenty minutes late," Tye rebutted, "but for you, that's on time."

Lexie motioned toward the old flowered chair. "Have a seat."

"Is that the hot seat?" Loretta's laugh mixed with tension.

"It is if you have something to hide. Will you give me a DNA sample and fingerprints without a court order?"

"I'm sure you'll get them one way or another. So go for it."

The procedures finished—the questioning started. Lexie stood behind Loretta's chair. "We can't catch this murderer without your cooperation."

"I want this guy caught more than you do. I can't even get my hair and nails done. My husband refuses to babysit me at the beauty salon. He turned into a prison guard when you told him to keep an eye on me."

Lexie nodded, "I'm glad he realized this is a life or death situation."

"Who murdered your friends?" Tye demanded.

"If I knew, I would've told you."

Lexie pushed, "I think you know, but you've chosen not to tell."

"That's ridiculous. Don't pull your cop psychology on me—telling me I know, when I don't."

Lexie confronted, "You do know that one secret."

Loretta straightened and leaned forward. "You're acting like you know something in the hopes I'll spill my guts."

"I know your secret—the abortion." Lexie thought that Loretta's look was best described as horror. Her eyes widened, then almost closed. Her hands clenched the chair arms.

"Who told you that?"

"Jamie said that your teammates knew and covered for you."

Loretta screeched, "That evil witch!"

Tye clamped his gaze on her. "Do you know anyone who'd punish you and the others for causing the baby's death?"

Loretta's face puffed with emotional venom. "You and your girlfriend accuse me of killing a baby? I'm sure she forgot to mention *her* secret."

"What secret is that?" Lexie asked calmly.

"I wasn't the only one who got pregnant. Jamie delivered her babies the summer *before* our senior year. I would've been pregnant through basketball season and missed the best year of my life. Everyone thought Jamie attended a basketball camp but she was in Missouri with her aunt, birthing—guess whose babies?"

Loretta pointed a finger at Tye. "You're a prime suspect. Jamie gave away your twin sons. That's reason for a childless man to murder his lover and all her co-conspirators. Jamie gave away your sons—gone forever. Doesn't that make you homicidal?"

"SHUT UP," Tye's fist clutched inches from her face.

Lexie intervened, "Who knew about Jamie's pregnancy?"

"Team knew, and her dad. He said she was too young, and Tye too wild, to take care of a family. All Daddy Jim cared about was winning the basketball championship so he'd be Coach of the Year." Acid dripped from Loretta's words.

"Anyone angry about Jamie giving away the babies?" Lexie determined to find an answer.

"Why don't we call them your nephews," Loretta's words stung. "No one seemed upset about the adoptions. The only one who might be angry at this late date is your childless brother."

"Perhaps a possibility—if he'd known," Lexie defended.

"Maybe he found out," Loretta accused, "and now he's killing everyone who took his sons from him. Tye, is Jamie next on your list?"

"Trust me, if I was the killer, you'd die next."

"Your deputy threatened me—lock him up."

"By the way, Jamie didn't tell me about the abortion, Mariah did. You betrayed Jamie—not the other way around."

"Mariah!" Loretta yipped. "Of all the people to divulge other people's secrets!"

"What was Mariah's secret?"

"Ask her what we found out that night by the lake. Ask her why we swore to keep our mouths shut. Let her tell you her own secret—that two-faced bitch!" Loretta's voice went from a strained monotone to a screech.

"Why ask her? Just tell me," Lexie ordered.

"I'm better than she is. I promised, and I'll keep my word."

"Don't you get it, Loretta? She set you up. Your motive is to shut up the team before your husband, and everyone else in this town, judges you."

Her words fired out. "Her father is the one who hired the midwife who did my abortion. Mariah's apparently setting him up, too. You can check my alibis. Oh, there is one more thing you might ask Daddy Sean. What happened to his son?"

Lexie took the bait. "What does his dead son have to do with this?"

"Dead? Maybe—maybe not," her tone teased. "Stop interrogating an innocent woman, and start asking Mariah and Sean all your questions. After all, her husband is running for president and her secrets may ruin both their futures. I'm leaving, unless you're arresting me." Loretta walked with each arm encircling a bag as she moved toward the door. One side of her hair stuck out which added to her freaked-out appearance. She rushed into the damp April weather.

"Dear, God." Delia's head shook, "All these dirty secrets: I thought they were a bunch of sweet basketball girls."

Lexie verbally conveyed her *to do* list. "We have three secrets to investigate. Starting tomorrow, we'll bring in anyone, and everyone, who had anything to do with the team. That includes coaches, junior varsity players, teachers, boyfriends, and family members. Delia, take a lunch break. When you get back, we'll schedule meetings over the next two to three days."

Delia retrieved her purse from the closet, "I'll be back in half an hour."

Tye headed toward the door, "I'll be at Jamie's house."

"Do you want to talk about the boys?"

"No," Tye answered flatly.

"Stop at Beth's on the way. See if you can get more out of her, based on the information Loretta gave us."

"Will do. I'll phone if Beth says anything interesting."

Lexie watched him leave. There was desperation in his eyes. She didn't know what to say or do to help him. The thought of having two nephews lifted her spirits. A thought she wouldn't share with her brother anytime soon.

Chapter Thirty-Four

Tye heard, and felt, the bump-bumpity-bump of the flat tire a mile out of town. He lifted the jack from the toolbox and pumped up the truck. The sweat beaded on his face. His shirt stuck to his damp skin so he took it off and threw it in the bed.

Loretta's words didn't leave his head. Somewhere he had two sons. He felt strange, as if he was a different person—he was cut off from an important part of his life. *Do they ever wonder about their father? The adoptive parents may never have told them that their father is alive.* He switched the jack for his shirt and resumed his trip to Beth's house.

Flower boxes on the windows, rows of daffodils by the front sidewalk, and a yellow porch swing all added to the appeal of the small house. Beth opened the door before he knocked.

"Darren is napping, I'd like to talk out here," Beth requested.

"Fine with me."

"What else do you want? I've already answered Lexie's questions."

"We have new information. I hope you'll contribute, since you weren't the one who told the secrets first. You kept your promise."

"What secrets?" Beth stammered.

"Loretta's abortion, Jamie's twins, and what you learned about Mariah the night after the championship game."

"You know now. Why are you still asking me

questions?"

"Because I don't know enough to figure out who wants you dead. Did anyone know about the pregnancies? Who was angry or upset?"

Beth bit her lower lip. "We were the only ones who knew."

"You don't think either of them killed to keep your mouths shut."

"No."

"Was Mariah's secret worth poisoning a few old teammates?"

Her voice softened, "You really don't know what happened?"

"What are you hiding, Beth?"

"I've got nothing else to say. Leave me alone."

"Beth, you may die. Darren can't stay beside you every second of every day. Sooner or later, the killer will get you, too."

"Quit scaring my wife," Darren's scruff voice carried from inside the screen door to the front porch.

Tye shot back, "Don't you two get it? There's a murderer waiting for his chance to kill again. Darren, if you want your wife alive, convince her to tell the truth." He paused, hoping for a response. When none came, he added, "You know where to reach me if you come to your senses." He turned and walked away. He was sick of people and their secrets.

Tye purposely drove slowly to Jamie's house. The correct words didn't form in his mind. *What does a man say to a woman who gave away his sons? Maybe I shouldn't say anything to her ever again.* Hollering and throwing objects might be his best recourse, or cursing and pointing. He didn't have the energy for any of the alternatives. The news sucked out his spirit.

Only one light was visible from her house. He knocked. Jamie opened the door and looked at him, saying nothing. There was a meekness and mildness about her that he'd never seen before. He felt his anger deflate into sadness.

Jamie left the door opened and walked into the living room. She sank into the sofa. Tye followed and sat on a chair directly across from her. Pulling the chair forward, he was within two feet, looking squarely into her face.

Jamie took a deep breath, "Loretta phoned."

"I figured."

"I've never known Loretta to be apologetic. Sounded like she genuinely wanted forgiveness."

"Not easy for someone who thinks she's perfect," Tye retorted.

Neither spoke for a long moment.

"Did you see the babies?"

"No, I didn't want to see them." Jamie's face was drawn. Her body slumped forward.

"Were they okay?"

"The nurse said they were healthy boys. They weighed between four and five pounds each."

Tye choked out the most important question, "Who adopted them?"

"I don't know."

Silence hung, then Tye asked, "I wonder if they had lots of dark hair?" He stared at the wall. "Indian babies usually do."

"I don't understand why you're not yelling! Why aren't you telling me what a horrible person I am? I gave away our sons. You should never forgive me." A sob escaped with her words.

"I love you, Jamie. I have for years. But I thought you didn't love me. You always kept your distance. Is this why?"

"If I married you, I owed you the truth and I couldn't bear to tell. I knew what I did was unforgivable."

"You were barely more than a kid, and I was a wild Indian—not exactly parenting material." He sat beside her and held both of her hands in his.

"Can you forgive me, Tye?"

"I already have." He held her close as she let the sadness erupt into heart wrenching sobs.

"We'll find them, Jamie, to make sure they're safe and loved."

"I want to see their faces," she moaned, clutching his hands.

"Me, too. We'll start looking tomorrow. Where will your father be in the morning?"

"At school finishing his paperwork for the year."

Tye came up with a quick plan. "I'll meet you at the front door of the high school at nine. We'll see what we can find out."

"Dad isn't likely to tell you anything."

Tye suppressed his anger. "We'll see about that. He owes us an explanation and we'll get it."

"If you threaten him, he won't give us anything," Jamie warned.

"I won't get angry. I'm a father who wants to learn about his sons."

Jamie's eyes had a glimmer of hope. "I'll meet you there."

Chapter Thirty-Five

The mirror reflected Tye's sleepless night. Forcing himself to look presentable, he put on a button-down shirt and khaki slacks. Pulling his hair firmly back, he secured it with a leather tie. Since time allowed, he polished his old boots and scraped the dirt from yesterday's lawn work from under his fingernails. He hoped he looked like father material. Maybe Jim would realize that the wild kid was long gone and give Tye a break— for a change.

The clock moved so slowly that Tye left to keep himself occupied. Even though he was thirty minutes early, he wasn't surprised that Jamie sat on the front school steps waiting for him. He hadn't seen her in a dress for years, but there she was in blue. Her long brown hair flowed around her shoulders instead of the usual tight ponytail. He approached the steps, "Did you tell him we were coming?"

"I thought the element of surprise might be an advantage."

"I agree," Tye reached out his hand and helped her up.

"This is it," she said.

"Yes, the first step in finding our sons."

They walked down the steps into the locker room. Jim talked on the phone about the gym renovation. He didn't hear them come up behind him.

Turning around, his eyes met Jamie's. He muttered into the phone, "Gotta go."

The two sat without an invitation.

"Dad, please help us find our sons."

Jim pointed a finger at Tye. "Don't you remember the pain that jerk caused us?"

"I could've stopped it, but I didn't want too."

Jim lifted a fist into the air and bellowed, "If he had a brain he would've put on a condom! He should've taken care of you."

Tye spoke, "You're right. I didn't consider the consequences. I was too stupid to think of anyone but myself. I'm sorry for the pain I caused your family."

Jim's fist lowered as if Tye's words depleted his power. "An apology doesn't change anything." Sweat paths formed down the sides of his face.

"Dad, it happened nineteen years ago. Surely you can forgive us."

"I don't know if I can. I've hated him for so long, that's all I know how to do."

Jamie pleaded, "We won't disrupt their lives if they're doing well. What if they aren't? What if they need our family?"

"I think about them, too—wonder if they'd be basketball stars like you. Maybe I'd had another championship season if the boys were here."

Anger tightened Tye's chest. *Jim's selfishness was why the boys were sent away in the first place.*

"Tell us everything you know," Jamie begged.

"A Missouri attorney named Alex Thomas arranged private adoptions. Your Aunt Chelsea knew him from church. He found a couple that wanted a boy. They paid for everything including attorney fees."

Anguish invaded Tye's tone, "They just took one baby?"

"Thomas claimed that the new parents didn't want two

sons."

Jamie choked back tears, "Who adopted the other boy?"

Jim shook his head, "Don't know."

Her words cracked, "What does that mean?"

"Dr. Carr said his daughter and son-in-law weren't able to have a child. He thought they'd consider adoption. I gave him Thomas' name and told him to contact the lawyer directly if his daughter was interested in the boy."

"Dr. Carr is the one who told me I was pregnant."

"What's his daughter's last name?" Tye asked.

"Didn't ask, 'cause I didn't care."

Tye felt sweat beads erupt on his forehead. "Where's Dr. Carr?"

Jim answered while looking at Jamie, "He lives on a farm forty miles north of town. The place with old plows decorating the front yard."

"I know where that is," Tye stood.

Jim's words boomed, "Hold up, man! Carr may never have contacted Thomas."

"Do you remember anything else, Dad?"

Jim pounded the desk, "I've said too much already. Someone took care of them for years. Don't disrupt their lives. You said you'd leave them alone; mind your own business."

Tye looked back as his foot touched the first step. Jamie leaned down and hugged the man who gave away his sons. He jogged up the stairs before a burst of anger could fire from his mouth. He waited for Jamie at the front door. She didn't recognize what he was feeling, or if she did, she wasn't ready to acknowledge it.

"What now?" she asked.

"Ask your aunt where Thomas is. Find out if she knows what happened to our sons. I'll question Carr at his farm."

"You know what my dad said."

"I don't give a damn what your old man said!"

She abruptly turned away, and jogged to her vehicle.

"She shouldn't have given that demon a hug," Tye muttered.

Twenty minutes on the highway, a right turn, then a rocky, curvy road led to Carr's place. Tye doubted a vehicle could get near the man's house after a hard rain. It was set on a hill. Antique plows still decorated the front yard.

Tye mentally searched for the right words to convince Carr that the boys deserved to learn that their father was alive. He didn't desert them nineteen years before. Many words came to mind during his long drive, but none of them fit together right. To beg, to threaten, or to offer money were alternatives. However, none of them seemed correct.

Tye walked across Carr's yard. It was almost devoid of grass because huge shade trees kept the sun from reaching the ground. Small tornados of dust sprang around his feet as his pace quickened. The old house was recently painted. The red shutters and porch were a sharp contrast to the white frame. His fist formed to attack the door. He loosened his grip so the knock wouldn't frighten the old man.

Tye heard movement from within. The shuffling sound reached the front door.

Carr opened the door. "Aren't you Nodin Wolfe's boy?"

"Yes, sir, I am." Tye held out his hand to meet the old man's weak grasp.

"Your dad was a good man, a hard worker. Tragic the way we lost him. That murder was a nightmare."

"It was a hard time," Tye confirmed.

Carr opened the door and pushed his walker over the threshold to the porch, then motioned Tye toward the swing.

"What are you doin' in these parts, boy? Did someone rustle cows?"

"No. I have a personal problem and I need your help."

Carr's wrinkles deepened around his mouth. "What's that boy?"

"Jim Evans told Jamie and me that your daughter was interested in adopting one of our twin boys."

Tye watched as Carr circled his tongue around his lips and fingered the bar on his walker. "True," he finally answered.

"Did she adopt one?"

"I told that lawyer he shouldn't split up those boys. My daughter and her husband wanted both of them. Thomas said it was one, or none. I know those folks paid him big bucks for gettin' them the other boy."

"Did you hear the name of the other family?"

"No. Thomas was secretive. Probably afraid someone would mess up his money deal."

"Did your daughter adopt one of my sons?"

"My daughter and her husband died in a plane crash two years ago. That damn crash almost took my entire world."

"Was their son in the crash?"

"No, thank God. He was spending the weekend with a friend. He's the only family I've got left in the world." Carr peered into the distance. "When you're eighty-six, sometimes you say more than you mean to."

"My son is alive and well?" Tye couldn't contain his excitement.

Carr's eyes lit, "That he is. A fine young man and the joy of my life."

"Where is he?"

"Can't say. He doesn't know about the adoption or his brother. You mess with his life and you'll tarnish his past and ruin my future."

"All I care about is his well-being," Tye said solemnly.

Carr's voice cracked, "He's fine as long as you stay out of his life."

"You're an old man, Carr. Will he have any family when you die?"

The man's body stiffened, "Nope, he won't."

"You're willing to leave him alone in the world even though he has a mom, dad and brother?"

"His mom and dad died."

"I know they were his parents. They loved and took care of him. But he shouldn't be left without a family when you die." Tye's voice was an up and down ebb of emotion.

A deep choking sound came from Carr's throat, "Maybe."

Tye promised, "I won't say anything until after you die. I don't want to hurt him—or you."

Worry labored Carr's words. "He may not forgive me when he finds out I never told him the truth."

"Is he that kind of boy?"

"No. He'd forgive me. I know he would."

The sound of an engine struggling up the hill filled the air with pops and rattles. An old Ford truck pulled beside the house. A young man jumped out the door like a jack-in-the-box.

"He's home early." Apprehension tightened the old

man's words. The lanky young man joined them. "This is my grandson, Adam."

Tye leaned forward but his body wouldn't rise. He felt tears surface and his heartbeat became so rapid that he thought the organ would jump from his chest.

"Are you okay, Mr. Wolfe?" Adam sounded concerned.

Tye nodded, "Choked for some reason."

"Man you look pale. Gramps, I know him. I write stories about the sheriff's department for the paper."

"And good stories they are, my boy."

"You know Gramps?" Adam patted the old guy's shoulder.

"My father knew him. I came over to talk him into selling one of those antique plows, but they aren't for sale."

"They're each like one of my children. I keep them all in my family."

"I understand. If you ever change your mind, please call me…anytime."

Tye grabbed the swing chain and pulled himself up. "I better get a move on. Glad to see you again." He grasped his son's hand for a few seconds.

"You, too. I'll bug you about another story soon."

"Bug away," Tye smiled, then walked dazed to his truck.

Tye looked through the glass as Adam helped Carr into the house. The boy's arm was wrapped affectionately around the old man's shoulder.

Tye drove without noticing the bumps and curves. Pulling off the road, he parked in a clearing surrounded by trees. Heaving sobs controlled his body. They were a welcome release from the emotion of finding his son. The upheaval left as quickly as it came. He sat without movement for an hour. He didn't know how he'd pretend that Adam wasn't his son.

Back on the highway, he drove toward Jamie's to learn how her search unfolded. He determined not to repeat Carr's story. He knew that one son was well and loved which was all he and Jamie said they cared about. These two things he'd confirm without telling the whole truth.

Tye knocked impatiently on Jamie's door. No long conversations—in and out. Since he blew up at the school, there was a chance she wasn't talking to him at all.

Jamie swung the door open. "Did you find out anything?" Come on in." They ended up on opposite ends of the sofa.

"I found out that Carr's daughter did adopt our son and he is alive and well."

"Where is he? When can we meet him?" Jamie's words gushed.

"Carr doesn't want us involved. I told him that we only cared that our sons were doing well."

"But I want to see him," Jamie insisted.

"I promised Carr that I wouldn't disrupt the boy's life if he told the truth, and I won't. What did your Aunt Chelsea say?"

"Chelsea said that attorney, Thomas, left town about fifteen years ago and no one has heard from him since. She didn't know who ended up with the babies. Both of them went out of state, she thought, but she wasn't sure about that either."

"Sounds like a dead end. We'll look until we find out he's okay, too."

"What next?"

"As soon as the reunion is over, we'll search for

Thomas," Tye promised. "He's the only link we have with our boy."

"Didn't Carr say anything else about our son? What he looks like? What he likes to do?"

"He wants us out of his life. Our son was never told he was adopted, or a twin." Tye gave her a quick kiss, and escaped before Jamie's questions resumed.

Emotions bubbled up in his head: guilt, joy, sadness, happiness, pride, fear, and regret. He wasn't capable of putting a name on what he felt after this day of meeting his son and telling Jamie half-truths.

Chapter Thirty-Six

Lexie was tired of making phone calls. It was unbelievable how many people were associated in one way or another with the girls' basketball team. Of course, people had died and probably a third moved away. She'd decide whether or not to hunt them down after she interviewed thirty-two locals. "Go home, Delia. It's been tedious with one phone call after another."

"You talked me into it." Delia stood but her body didn't continue forward movement. "I'm stiff as can be. This gettin' old is for the birds."

"You just sat too long," Lexie assured her.

"I'll be here tomorrow, bright and early." Delia limped toward the door.

"Neither bright, nor early, sound good to me," Lexie joked.

Alone, Lexie listed questions for potential witnesses. Five o'clock moved to nine. The sound, at first, was a rustling, like an animal near the back door, but then it intensified. She startled to survivor mode.

She slid from the chair, and knelt on the floor behind the desk. Her chest heaved as she retrieved a gun. *Has the murderer gotten so anxious to kill me that he risked coming into town?*

The noise became human babble with an occasional "damn" thrown in. The back door flung open. Drunken Clay lost his balance and stumbled.

Lexie rose with her gun drawn. "I should shoot you. A

drunk deputy is useless."

Dirty blond curls covered his eyes and he showed no awareness of her gun or words.

"Crawl to the cell," she ordered, then pushed him in the right direction.

He lumbered bent over, toward the cot, then fell sideways onto its surface.

"This will keep you, and the public, safe for tonight." The bang of the cell door didn't faze him.

The drive home was a welcome reprieve from her long day and liquored up deputy. She remembered the fear Clay's sounds provoked in her. Somehow, she brushed aside the fact that someone wanted her dead. Fearful, she checked the door locks one more time then crawled into bed. Her hand reached under the pillow beside her. The gun's feel gave her comfort and confidence.

Chapter Thirty-Seven

Lexie's phone rang before the alarm clock woke her. Clay bellowed behind the clear sound of Tye's voice.

"Sis, may I release Clay from jail? Say the word and I'll keep him in for life."

"Release him if he's sobered up."

"He's madder than a wet hornet."

"He'll get over it, if not, he's certainly welcome to quit."

Tye chuckled, "A message I'll pass on. When will you arrive?"

"Around eight. See you then."

Lexie's mind clicked off plans for the day as she drove. The reunion was ten days away. It was imperative that she figure out who the murderer was before he blended in with other visitors. Keeping Jamie, Beth, Loretta, and Mariah alive was a frightening responsibility.

She'd question people of interest today, tomorrow, and Friday. Her list included Jamie's father and Mariah's father. She was most curious about Sean's answers. Hopefully, DNA and fingerprints results would arrive soon.

Parking the patrol car at the rear of the building, she entered through the back door. Gary King was seated across from Tye. She purposely scheduled him first to get it over with. Gary nodded. *At least he's not lunging toward my throat.*

"Have you found a suspect?" Gary grumbled.

"We have clues, but no answer. Heather left a message that an old friend from high school was visiting. That was the morning she died. I believe the killer was associated with your senior class. That's why Abbey felt safe meeting him, or her. We know that Loretta, Jamie, and Mariah have secret pasts. Did you hear rumors when you were at school? Did Abbey ever tell you anything about those three?"

"Abbey didn't like their personalities, but she never accused them of bad stuff. What did they do?"

"We can't let that out," Tye answered.

"Are you finished with me? I'm late for work."

Tye shook his hand. Gary avoided contact with Lexie.

The morning was one person after another who knew nothing about team problems. No one admitted to hating any player, or knowing anyone who did.

Before the trail of witnesses commenced at one o'clock, Lexie sent Delia and Tye out to lunch.

"Bring me a hamburger and…" Lexie began but stopped when the phone rang. She waved them out the door.

"This is Bryce from OSBI. The tube prints didn't match any you sent. The ones that Interpol sent on Mariah Haverty didn't match either. Also, the print didn't match any of the criminals we have on file. No DNA on the lip-gloss. It was never used."

"I appreciate the heads up."

"Should make it easier for you. At least you can rule out those four women. I'll send results back quick if you get other prints," Bryce promised.

"Sure does help. Thanks." *That was a lie.* She shut off the phone. She had nothing and it was looking more and more like the lip gloss didn't belong to the murderer.

Tye returned with a hamburger and fries instead of her hoped for salad.

"OSBI phoned. If that lip gloss belonged to the killer, then Loretta, Jamie, Mariah, and Beth are in the clear."

"What else?"

"Interpol sent Mariah's fingerprints to Bryce. Of course, there was no DNA testing that far back. But we do have a hair I pulled off her brush."

"I hope something breaks in the next couple of days," Tye said gravely. "We're going to be 'up a creek without a paddle' as Grandpa used to say."

"I'll question Jim and Sean while you interview your high school gang." Lexie smiled at the prospect of escaping the office.

Tye mumbled, "Thanks so much Sheriff Wolfe. Nothing like a few more hours asking the same questions over and over to people who don't have answers."

"Be optimistic, Deputy Wolfe. Maybe one of the next ten will remember something."

"Right, Sheriff. I should've encouraged you to quit when you threatened to."

"Too late, big brother." Lexie was glad to leave the office and the repetitious questions behind.

Jim was her first stop. Perhaps he was the friend from high school who Heather mentioned. He was fifty-seven, but his tall lean body and head of curly brown hair made him look ten years younger. Still the school basketball coach, she found him in his basement office. Three 8 x 10 photos of basketball teams with statistics attached were lined up in front of him.

Jim looked up when Lexie entered, "How's it going?"

"Not well. Jamie, Beth, Loretta, and Mariah are at risk and my clues don't fit together."

"I asked Jamie to stay with her mom and me, but she won't do it. Told me she's a big girl. What can I do for you?"

"Fill me in on Jamie's pregnancy."

Red tones crept into his facial lines. "What pregnancy?"

"You know—the twins. The ones you gave away."

"Don't say it like that. Good people adopted them. Your brother knocked her up and he sure as hell wasn't father material. No scholarship or championship team if Jamie kept those babies. She deserved her senior year."

"And you, Jim, did you deserve that Coach of the Year trophy?"

He glared, "Yes, I did. What I did was for the best. Those babies were better off and so was Jamie."

"This makes you look bad, Jim. Giving away grandbabies doesn't sound good. Who knew about the twins?"

"The varsity basketball players."

"Quite a coincidence those women are dying one by one."

The vein on Jim's f0rehead popped up. "What are you implying?"

She continued her push. "That you don't want your baby giveaway to go public. Your reputation as a great guy would suffer. Your wife lost her only grandchildren. That's a motive for murder. Your image as a good husband and an outstanding coach tarnished forever."

Angry words sparked, "I didn't hurt those girls! They were like daughters."

"Give me a DNA sample and your fingerprints to prove you're as innocent as you claim," Lexie snarled.

His forehead vein bulged. "Get your evidence and get out. I don't appreciate your accusations."

Lexie put on gloves and swabbed the inside of his cheek, then got fingerprints. The silence loomed during her tasks. She left without another word passing between them.

Sean sat on his front porch swing. His gaze lifted from the hanging plant to Lexie's face as she walked up the steps. His facial wrinkles were more imbedded than usual. His eyes drooped.

"Help me, Sean. I can't figure out the purpose of these murders. I can't live with myself if the other girls end up like Abbey."

Sean petted his dog that inserted its head under the arm rail of the swing."

"Can't help you with that," Sean spoke slowly as if thinking it through.

"Can't or won't?" Lexie challenged.

"What I think has nothin' to do with the murders. Just an old man's imaginings."

"But what if your thoughts are correct? Will you risk your daughter's life?"

"Don't be hateful with an old man. I told you, it's imaginings, not facts."

"Is it a fact you arranged for Loretta's abortion?"

His hand froze on the dog's head.

"You have a secret, Sean, that can damage your son-in-law's presidential campaign. It doesn't look good for a right-to-lifer candidate to have a father-in-law who planned a minor's illegal abortion."

He wheezed. "You don't understand."

Lexie softened her tone, "Then explain, Sean."

"Loretta was irrational when she found out about the pregnancy. Mariah told me the girl might commit suicide if anyone found out. The town gossip would've ruined her and soiled the team's reputation. You know how people gossip here, Lexie."

"Who was the father?"

"They never said."

"Surely you have a guess, Sean."

"Mariah said he was from Tulsa."

Lexie probed, "Did you believe her?"

Sean shook his head no.

"Who performed the abortion?"

Sean fingered a button on his flannel shirt. "A midwife in Little Rock."

"Her name?" Lexie scooted her chair closer.

"She said it was Savannah something, but I doubted it."

"Anyone assist her?"

"Don't know. The girls and I waited in a restaurant across the street from the old motel where it was done."

Lexie continued, "Which girls were with you?"

"Mariah, Jamie, Beth, Abbey, Heather, Tina and Terri were all there. It was near Mariah's birthday. We told the parents it was a weekend birthday celebration. No one was suspicious."

Weren't you afraid the truth would come out?"

"At first, but I did what I thought was best."

Harshness invaded her tone. "Since you have a military background, I'm sure you know you're a suspect. You certainly have a motive."

His distress was evident. "I know this looks bad, but you'll waste your time if you investigate me."

"And then there's the other secret—Mariah's."

The old man looked stunned. "What are you talking

about?"

"Don't play dumb with me, Sean."

"Mariah had a hard time back then. Her Mom died when we lived there. Sometimes she acted strange, but she was depressed," Sean explained.

"Did she ever tell you what her team members found out that night by the lake?"

He snapped, "I wouldn't put credence in anything drunk teenagers said."

"Sean, will you voluntarily let me take a DNA sample and fingerprints?"

"Anything, to be left alone."

Her work completed, she left Sean on the front porch fingering the button his nervous fingers pulled from his shirt.

Driving back to the office, her head filled with questions she couldn't answer. A lack of answers could result in four more deaths.

Tye rolled his eyes and shook his head when Lexie walked into the office.

"Doesn't look like you've had a happy day." Lexie smiled.

"That's not the half of it," Tye complained. "Nobody knew anything, but some of them pretended they did. Of course, everyone has a theory. There was only once that I didn't suppress a yawn. I'm proud of that accomplishment."

Lexie held up her Coke as if in toast, "And well you should be proud."

"How about you?" Tye queried.

"At first, we had no clues or suspects and now, we've got too many. It's like having three puzzles with the pieces all mixed together. No way to know which one needs worked first in order to catch the murderer."

"What're you thinking?"

Lexie responded, "It looks bad for Sean. He has the best motive for killing team members, because of the potential impact on Mariah's future."

"Mariah and her husband both have the same motive as Sean. Anyway, he isn't physically capable of murdering people," Tye reasoned.

Lexie continued, "Then there's people who have a motive if they found out the truth. There's the father of Loretta's baby and that guy's family. Maybe the midwife decided to shut up people who knew about her side practice. Anyway, it's a long line of connections that go nowhere."

"I didn't find out anything today that I didn't already know." Tye sounded frustrated. "I did discover that teenage girls could keep secrets."

"They had good reason with their championship season on the line. I assume that's why they never told anyone."

"Does that mean I can cancel the interviews tomorrow?"

"Good try, big brother. Think of it as a challenge. Discover if you can make it through without any yawns at all."

"There's a goal!"

"Lexie, phone," Delia called.

"Bryce at OSBI. Sheriff Wolfe, none of the three Washington hair samples were from Mariah. One under the name of her assistant, Wade, and two matched Donovan."

"Okay. I'll get a sample from Mariah. Sorry for the mix-up."

Lexie slammed the phone onto the receiver. "I messed up the DNA samples from DC. I pulled hairs from two brushes thinking I had Mariah's brush and her husband's. Instead I ended up with two of his. Now I must go back and get official samples. It'll give me the opportunity to question her eye-to-eye before the reunion—a good thing."

"No way are you getting on an airplane." Tye's tone was firm. "Someone might blow you up this time."

"Be careful. You're acting like you love your sister." Delia's mouth curved into a wide smile.

"Don't get mushy," Tye warned. "I'm just too lazy to do this job alone."

"Not to worry. I'll ask Red to fly me."

"Good," Tye sounded relieved.

"This guy's awfully quiet," Delia commented, "do you think he's given up?"

"I bet he's waiting on the reunion. We're giving him the perfect opportunity to murder again."

"That sounds creepy," Delia shivered.

"Yes, but it's also our best, and maybe only, opportunity to catch him. We'll know he's here with us."

Delia shook her head. "I don't think that's a good thing."

"Delia, go by Beth's in the morning. Write down everything they have planned for the reunion from Friday night through Sunday: times, locations, and speakers. Find out when the four possible victims will be in close proximity. Make a reunion list of everyone and where they are staying. Include cell phone numbers and spouses' names."

"I'll phone and tell her I'm dropping by," Delia responded.

As soon as Delia was off the phone, Lexie picked up hers.

"Red, you said to call if I needed assistance, and this is

it."

"I hope you need me in a physical way?" Red teased.

"No. Sorry."

"I was afraid of that. What's the deal?"

"Will you fly me to Washington tomorrow?"

"Visiting the hunk?" Red sounded suspicious.

"Can't stand the sight of the jerk. If I trusted him, I wouldn't go. I'd ask him to question Mariah."

"I'm convinced. I'll phone you when arrangements are finalized."

Ten minutes later Red was back on the line. "DC airport said we couldn't fly in until the afternoon. Meet me at ten o'clock at our airfield."

"Thanks," Lexie acknowledged.

Her directions commenced before the phone hit its cradle. "I'll cover for you in the morning, Delia. Tye, have Clay help you work out guard duties in the gym. Also, phone the highway patrol and ask if they'll send extra manpower."

"Will do. Clay may not show," Tye reminded her.

"Did you talk to him about the drinking?"

"No, he was just blowing off steam like young guys do," Tye responded.

"Your excuse for him aside—that's not the deputy image I want."

Clay entered the door as Lexie finished her sentence. He was closely shaven and his uniform neatly pressed.

"Now, *that's* the image I like," Lexie remarked.

"What?"

"Referring to a previous conversation," Lexie said. "I'm out of here. You know how to reach me."

"Okay," Clay blurted. "Sorry about the other night."

"It's over," Lexie said. "Tye will fill you in, Clay. See you all tomorrow."

Chapter Thirty-Eight

The morning sun blurred Lexie's vision as she drove from the office to the small airport outside of town.

Her thoughts documented the morning events. She reviewed the interviews she and Tye conducted. Delia's discourse on the 'when, where and who' of the twentieth reunion drug on for almost an hour. On one hand, she was glad the reunion was only a few days away. The end of the investigation was in sight. On the other hand, she couldn't live with herself if the demon murdered one, or more, of the women right under her nose. She looked forward to the four-hour flight to Washington, D.C., with Red.

"Howdy, stranger," he called as she approached the plane.

"Look who's talking. Did you forget where I work?"

"I'm fixing up Dad's old place between plane trips." He kissed her lips. "Get in, girl, or we'll be late for your date."

The flight seemed like an hour, instead of four. It was a lovely clear day. Red filled the time with animated stories about his customers and house renovation.

On the ground, they rented a car and headed for the Toleson Mansion.

"I've got my cell phone right beside me, and I'll wait in front," Red assured her.

"I don't think this will take over an hour."

"If its much more than that, I'll put on my cape and fly through the door."

Lexie grinned, "Superman Red flying to my rescue!"

The maid opened the door before Lexie rang the bell.

"Come quickly. Ms. Mariah has a dinner party tonight. She's upset that you're late."

When Lexie entered the sitting room, Mariah's face scrunched in disgust. "I don't have much time left to talk."

"I'm only ten minutes late. It's impossible to predict flight time, airport, and traffic congestion." Lexie added malice to her tone.

"Yes, yes, I know," Mariah's voice lost its edge.

"Tell me what your team members learned by the lake twenty years ago."

"It's so embarrassing. I was a stupid teenager. If the story gets out, people will think I'm a thief. The jokes on the late shows will focus on locking up everything at the White House if I become First Lady."

"You stole something?" Lexie clarified.

"Yes, a diamond heart necklace. It was beautiful. When the sales lady talked to Heather, I dropped it in my purse."

"Then what happened?"

"That night, at the lake, Heather called me a thief and told the others. I made them swear never to tell. If they did, I had plenty of dirt to broadcast regarding them."

"Who was with you at the jewelry store?"

"Only Heather."

"I need a DNA sample and fingerprints." Lexie opened her kit.

"I don't want to be involved in this mess."

Lexie pulled the court order out of her bag and handed it to Mariah. *At least the hunk got that done. He had, however, refused to get an order for Donovan.*

Mariah's face squeezed in disgust after Lexie did the

mouth swab. One would've thought her fingers were being amputated instead of printed by the way her body stiffened. "Thanks for your time."

"It certainly wasn't pleasant."

"I could tell," Lexie's lips tightened. "This guy is probably long gone, but be vigilant. I'll see myself out."

As Lexie walked toward the gate, she felt watched. She stopped and visually scanned the area. The tall trees camouflaged much of the landscape. Picking up her pace, she jogged to the rental car.

"Let's go. This place gives me the creeps."

Red's foot pressed the gas. It was a fast beginning to the trip back to the airport. "How'd it go?"

"Not well. She was angry that I showed up again. My requests for DNA and fingerprints really sent her up the wall."

"Sounds suspicious."

"The only person who can verify her jewelry store story is dead, and the others haven't told Mariah's secret."

"Convenient," Red concentrated on the traffic.

Lexie pushed numbers into her cell phone.

"Loretta, the day after your team won the state championship, before your cookout, what did you all do?"

"How the hell do you expect me to know that?" Loretta whined.

"Try, please. Did any of you go out of town?"

"All I remember is that I was mad at Heather because she didn't help. She stayed in bed like she always did on the first day of her period. She showed up in time for the party and camping, however, which was suspicious."

"Thanks," Lexie hung up the phone.

"The fact that Loretta can hold a grudge for twenty years has turned into a blessing. Mariah spent an hour lying to me, or Heather lied to Loretta."

Red looked confused, "Sounds like your glad."

"If Mariah lied, it's a clue. Now I know which puzzle to put together first."

"Puzzles? I know I'm puzzled," Red chuckled.

"It's a long story. I'd rather talk about the reunion. Are you going?"

"Nope."

"Please reconsider. I can use an extra pair of eyes. Since you're alumni, no one will get suspicious about your presence."

"Anything for you, Sheriff Honey."

"Cute."

The flight back to Diffee drug on forever. At midnight, Lexie climbed into her soft bed and pulled covers to her chin. Her eyes closed sixty seconds after contact with the pillow and didn't open until seven the next morning.

Chapter Thirty-Nine

The light peeked in through the shades. She rolled over to avoid the intrusion. Her body was still, but her brain didn't slow down. Only one more week, and she had no doubt the murderer would arrive, assuming he didn't already live in Diffee. She rolled out of bed. Follow-up with Sean was the first thing on her schedule.

At 8 a.m., she parked the patrol car in front of his house. As usual, he sat on the porch swing. Dark circles underscored his eyes and his face was set in a frown.

"More questions?" He spewed as she approached the steps.

"Yes." Seating herself on the old rocker, she twisted around to face him.

"What happened that night at the lake? Your daughter lied. I can leak that she's a murder suspect. Then her husband's future, and hers, won't include a presidency."

"That's an evil thought."

"Vile perhaps, but deserving, since she lied about what happened at the lake. Why would she lie if she wasn't the murderer?"

Sean's shaking hand massaged his left temple.

Lexie pressed, "Why did she lie, Sean?"

"To protect her brother."

Lexie exclaimed, "Her dead brother?"

"Michael was mentally ill. When his girlfriend disappeared in Columbia, the locals accused him of murder. I got Michael out of the country before they killed him, or locked him up for the rest of his life. I nailed him in a wood box. The locals helped me carry him to the boat. They were all pleased when I told them he committed suicide. No one checked inside the coffin."

"Weird you got away with that."

"Not strange in Columbia. It was a whole different world then."

"Where is Michael?"

"I don't know. After he returned to the U.S., he changed his identity," Sean divulged.

"Mariah knows that he's still alive?"

"They make contact from time to time," Sean admitted.

"Why her and not you?"

"He hates me. He blamed me for his mother's death in Columbia. He said she didn't have a chance in that country without good medical care."

"Find a photo of Michael." He went inside the house and, after ten minutes, returned with a snapshot of his son.

Lexie walked away thinking that this puzzle had more pieces than she realized. She drove a few miles then pulled off the road.

She pushed Mariah's number into her cell phone. She regretted not seeing her face.

"Toleson residence," Wade answered.

"This is Sheriff Wolfe. Put Mariah on the line."

"It's that Sheriff," she heard him say in the background.

"What is it now?" Mariah commanded.

"Your father told me that Michael is still alive and makes contact with you."

"That old fool is crazy," Mariah snapped.

"Where is Michael buried?"

"Bogotá. That crazy man left him in the jungle," Mariah huffed.

"Where is your mother buried?"

"In Diffee—Sean brought her home."

"Why didn't he have Michael's body transported?"

"Sean thought it was a waste of money."

The sharpness of Mariah's words sent shivers down Lexie's arms. "Why did your father say that Michael is still alive?"

"I don't want to hear about that old fool's hallucinations. Hopefully, he's gone nuts over the guilt of my mom and brother dying in that horrid country. He cared about career advancement not his family."

"Do you have the location of Michael's burial site?" Lexie questioned.

"Of course," Mariah's tone flattened.

"Fax me the directions."

She grumbled, "Then will you leave me alone?"

"For now," Lexie replied. She gave Mariah her FAX number then pushed the phone's off button.

Delia was busy typing the reunion schedule when Lexie entered the office.

"What's up?" Tye's eyes widened.

"Let me make a call then I'll fill you in. You probably won't believe it. I'm not sure I do."

"Interesting," Tye replied.

Lexie dug the Interpol number out of her desk drawer then pushed the numbers in her phone. "This is Sheriff Lexie Wolfe from Diffee, Oklahoma. Send me prints from a Michael Haverty who was in Columbia with his father, Sean, ending around 1988."

"What's this about?" an official sounding voice asked.

"It's for a murder investigation. Sean Haverty reported that his son's death was faked to avoid retaliation and murder charges in South America. His sister, Mariah, said that he's dead and buried in Bogotá. If he's alive, he's probably the murderer I'm looking for. I'm hoping you have his fingerprints since his father was in security at the American Embassy. You've already sent me his sister's prints—Mariah Haverty."

"I'll check this out and get the information to OSBI."

"Bryce is handling the case for OSBI. Please hurry. There are others on the killer's list."

"Will do," the man hung up.

Tye's interest peaked, "What's going on?"

Lexie recounted her conversations from the morning.

"Unbelievable," was Tye's only response.

Lexie worried aloud, "My concern is that he won't show for the reunion because we're getting too close."

"Maybe he'll give up his vendetta for fear of falling in a trap." Delia's optimism didn't ring true.

Lexie frowned, "I don't understand why he's killing a bunch of women he never knew."

"Sounds like vengeance related to his sister," Tye speculated.

Lexie picked up the ringing phone. "Sheriff Wolfe here."

"This is Jenkins from Interpol. The information you requested was sent to Bryce at the OSBI office in Tulsa. You may access it through him."

"Thanks so much."

"Tye, how do you feel about a trip to Bogotá to see if Michael is still there—six feet under? It's the only way to know if Mariah is lying."

"Not exactly my idea of a vacation, but I'm ready for an adventure. Do you want Red to pilot?"

"Yes. He'll arrive any minute for our meeting. I want to make sure we all know our reunion assignments."

Clay, Red, and the highway patrol representative, Turner, arrived at about the same time.

Turner reached his hand to each in succession. He was a big burly guy with a dimple in his chin and a ready smile.

She asked Tye to coordinate the officers at the gym. Clay and Turner were assigned guard rotation at Loretta's house on Friday afternoon. The three women were doing prep work for the memorial service for their friends.

"Boss said we'll assign an officer to each woman once the festivities begin," Turner reported.

"That's great," Lexie replied. "Red, will you fly Tye to Bogotá tomorrow? Mariah's story must be verified."

"No can do. Phone Max Larson at Soaring Flights. His plane is better than mine and he speaks Spanish. Red mumbled, "Time to move on down the road. I've got work to do."

Lexie followed him out the door. "What happened to your promise about helping?"

"Only applied to the United States."

"You generally can't wait for an excuse to fly off into the sunset. Why are you deserting me?" Redness invaded Lexie's complexion.

"The last thing I'd ever do is desert you." His hand touched her shoulder.

She shrugged it off, "Is that why you won't go?"

"You got it. Someone tried to kill you. I'm not leaving

the country the same time as Tye."

"How often have I told you that I don't require a babysitter?"

"Way too many, so you might as well give it up," Red scowled, "don't waste your breath."

Lexie looked directly into his eyes. "Why are you such a pain in the ass?"

Red leaned over as if to kiss her. Instead, he turned her head sideways and whispered in her ear, "Because I love you." He quickly turned and left only his back for Lexie's glare.

She watched him walk away. Pretending that his declaration of love in Washington was a fluke wasn't easy now.

Tye contacted Max Larson about the Bogota' trip while she was outside.

Tye grabbed his coffee cup and jacket. "We're leaving at 6 a.m. I'll get packed then spend the night in Tulsa."

"I'll call ahead to inform the authorities." Lexie shook a finger at him, "Don't get in trouble."

"Not me, I'm too mild mannered."

"Like I believe that!" Lexie wrapped her arms around him.

"Don't get all mushy—makes me wonder what you're up to. I'll be back in a few days." Tye saluted as he exited.

"I'm out of here, too." Lexie patted Delia's back. "I'm making arrangements for a horseback ride early in the morning."

"Why?" Clay asked.

"It's time I brought Wilbur back to his cell."

"Clay should go with you." Delia stated.

"He'll need sleep after all-night duty. I arranged for Turner to work days while Tye is gone."

Turner nodded.

"I'll check in with you every hour so you can monitor what's happening. Wilbur doesn't have a history of shooting anyone. However, he might consider it a positive alternative to a return trip to prison."

Chapter Forty

Tye buckled his seatbelt, then visually sized up his pilot. Max Larson was probably in his early fifties, of medium height, with gray thinning hair. He assumed Max had plenty of money based on the diamond ring on his finger and the new airplane.

Max welcomed him aboard, "Hello."

"I appreciate you flying me on short notice." Tye settled into his red cushioned seat and fastened the seatbelt.

"I don't have anything better to do. I thought about flying to Paris for the weekend, but the thought of Columbia brought back old memories."

Tye's curiosity aroused. "You've been to Columbia?"

"I went as an interpreter for a professor from Wabash College in 1970." Max turned his attention toward maneuvering the plane down the runway.

Tye kept his mouth shut until the plane was airborne. He suspected Max was fairly new at flying. He preferred not to know the answer to that question.

"Was that professor collecting drugs in Columbia?" Tye joked after the plane leveled in the air.

Max grumbled, "That was before FARC got involved with cocaine to raise funds for their guerilla organization."

"What's FARC?"

"Revolutionary Armed Forces of Columbia. Those are the dirt bags who captured the three Americans last year."

"I do remember that story," Tye reflected.

"Columbia was a friendly place for Americans until FARC showed up. Now there are men who'll kidnap or murder you without a second thought. Especially, if they think they can get a ransom."

"In that case, I'm surprised you agreed to fly me."

Max gave him a sideways glance. "I'm landing and leaving, then I'll pick you up. San Jamiese del Guaviare is too dangerous for me. Strange that an American buried a loved one there."

"Sean worked for the American Embassy in Bogotá. He had something to hide. Probably why the body wasn't returned to the U.S."

"It certainly was the perfect place to hide a body," Max confirmed.

Tye switched subjects, "What were you doing in Columbia in 1970?"

"Collecting samples of slime molds."

Tye shook his head, "I've never heard of them."

"The professor thought they were fascinating because they're part plant and part animal on different life cycles. I collected dirt samples in film canisters for his research."

"To each his own." Tye studied the sky and became aware of an approaching storm.

"Thirty years since I was in that part of the world." Max paused and stretched his memory. "There were vines, monkeys, and snakes. Also, great fishing in the Amazon River. Mostly Peace Corp people around back then. We had some wild bus rides, weird hotel accommodations, and an occasional lizard on the supper table."

"Any cars around?" Tye asked.

"Some from the fifties. I visited one little Columbian gal. The family garage opened into their house. The car was parked in the house on the linoleum floor. Driving there was a gamble since they had almost no traffic signs."

"Sounds like an adventure."

"The most interesting thing happened the day we had to cross a river. There was no bridge to drive the Jeep over. These guys had us drive the Jeep into two canoes and they floated us across. Now that was an experience." Max's laughter filled the plane.

Tye joined in, "I hope they've built more bridges. I don't want to drown in a Jeep."

Max's tone became serious. "What you're doing is dangerous. You may never get back home. There are killers in the jungle. It's difficult to hire a guide, but I'll find you one before I fly to Villavicencio."

"What's so interesting there?"

"They had fabulous silver jewelry. I thought I'd get my wife a gift since I'm in the vicinity." Max's features tightened. "Get some rest while I concentrate on flying through this storm."

Tye faced the window. He concentrated on how to stay alive when he reached the destination. It wasn't possible to make plans since he didn't know what he was about to face. *Just play it by ear and pray a little.*

Chapter Forty-One

Lexie glanced at the clock on the truck's dashboard. It was 6:30 a.m. Tye was scheduled to take off thirty minutes before. The horse trailer made the truck difficult to steer. Many times she corrected the constant pull to the left.

Her mind persevered on Tye. *Maybe it was a mistake to send him.* She searched the Internet last night. She learned that in the 1990s, Columbia was one of the most deadly places in the world. According to the article in Wikipedia, it was not as dangerous now. That was her only solace.

She parked the truck and trailer beside Lulu's Country Store and Diner. Lulu's was where campers bought their bug spray, not to mention the essential beer and worms.

Lulu came around the corner as Lexie slid from the truck seat. "What are you up to, Lexie Girl?"

The head of the five-foot woman fit snuggly under Lexie's chin during the bear hug she delivered.

"I'm sneaking this truck and trailer out of the way, while I ride Flame."

"You sure ain't very secretive, girl, with that big rig."

"I never could fool you." Lexie patted Lulu's shoulder.

"No, and you still can't, even though I'm seventy-nine."

"Will I interfere with your customer parking if I park here?"

"It's fine, young'un. I bet you're goin' in the woods to arrest that drug sellin' fool, Wilbur."

"I really *can't* keep any secrets from you. Please don't tell anyone."

"I weren't going to," Lulu assured her with a hand

squeeze. "I keep my mouth shut about sheriff business. You can park here as long as you like. Do you need help gettin' that spotted horse out?"

"I can handle Flame. By the way, Turner from the highway patrol will arrive in a few minutes. He's my back-up today."

"I got to get back to fryin' eggs for them hungry men folk. You come in the cafe and tell me bye when you're finished chasin' Wilbur, so I can quit worrin' about you."

"I'll do it," Lexie promised.

Lexie backed Flame out of the trailer then saddled him. It was a mile ride to the river turnoff, but she didn't risk driving farther. The trailer's rattle on a rocky road wasn't going to warn Wilbur she was on her way. She easily put a foot in the stirrup, and swung her free leg over the saddle. Times like this made her glad Dad taught his daughter what he taught his son. She knew how to shoot straight, lasso, and ride better than most men. Her mother named her Alexandria, hoping for a girlie-girl. Margo ended up with a tomboy who liked to climb trees, and push male friends into the creek. Lexie wasn't the daughter her mother desired, and her disappointment was frequently evident.

Lexie held the reins loose which allowed Flame to follow his instinctive path beside the highway. The blacktop, and thoughts of her mother, ended as soon as she saw the dirt road that went toward Wilbur's house. Memories of Abbey's death crowded her mind.

Flame wasn't in any hurry. His gait slowed as they entered the woods. He found a path through the underbrush. His hoof beats blended perfectly with the sounds of nature. Splotches of blue sky were visible through the green canopy.

A hawk let out a squawk as she and Flame invaded its sanctuary. It soothed her to ride in this world untouched by human rigmarole.

Her eyes darted from side-to-side and her body twisted to look behind. Afraid she'd missed something because she allowed her mind to wander. However, everything belonged—except she and Flame.

Flame's steps quickened. The horse moved cautiously down an incline. Lexie leaned forward and stiffened to stabilize her body.

Flame stood in the creek and sucked water. Lexie watched the water flow swiftly down the stream, then pool into a large open area as if to rest before it returned to its hurried trip to the river. Brown stones were slick from the constant water flow.

Flame shook his head from side to side. Lexie wasn't sure if he was shaking off water, or if a minnow tickled his snout. She gave the reins a tug. Flame continued their journey across the creek and up the other bank. Thirty minutes later, she dismounted and tied Flame to a tree. She was pretty sure Wilbur's house was within five minutes walking distance.

A sound exploded in the distance; its echo rippled through the woods. She dropped to the ground and waited. Only the insects and the wind created noise. The gunshot came from the direction of Wilbur's place and wasn't meant for her.

Standing, she visually explored the surrounding area. Running forward, she avoided the branches that might pop and break under the pressure of her weight and create a path of sound for whoever fired the gun. As Lexie neared the house, she stooped and walked cautiously toward the back door.

"You SONOFABITCH!" A voice bellowed from within the house. "Next time I'm goin' shoot you through the head. I want my money. You ain't cheatin' me from what's rightfully mine."

"I ain't got it. My woman took it when she left."

"You lyin' bastard!" A staccato yell blasted from the same man. "I'm goin' beat the shit out of you!"

Lexie heard the sound of wood hitting the floor and Wilbur's high-pitched scream. She looked through the space between the curtains as the wind blew against them. She saw Wilbur tied to a chair that had fallen on its side. The sleeve of his shirt was wet with blood. His cousin, Toby, stood over him— a gun to the side of his head.

"I'm goin' kill you deader than a rock." Toby's voice was hoarse. The gun in his right hand shook. He stabilized it with his left hand. "Give it to me or be in hell tonight."

"I told you I ain't got your money." Lexie barely heard the words that Wilbur squeaked.

"You bastard!" Toby croaked. "Five, four, three, two—"

Lexie aimed her shot through the open window at Toby's right leg. The bullet hit its mark.

Toby dropped the gun, and grabbed his leg. A wild animal roar exploded out his mouth.

Lexie crashed through the back door.

Toby grabbed his gun. One shot ricocheted off the door near Lexie. He turned the gun to Wilbur's head. "YOU BASTARD! Get my money!"

Wilbur's face crunched into a mass of fleshy terror. Lexie fired the shot directly at Toby's chest and watched him fall.

Adrenaline shot through Lexie's body. She pulled the walkie-talkie from her backpack. The words came out fast, "Turner, call the med helicopter. I've got two wounded men here."

Turner's voice strained, "Are you okay?"

"Get officers here immediately."

While she untied Wilbur from the chair, she noted his pale face and glassy eyes. She wrapped a stained dishtowel around his wound then maneuvered him to the couch.

Toby's breathing was shallow, his pulse slow. She pressed a towel against his chest. It was soon saturated with blood. Droplets of blood sprinkled her as he coughed.

"That asshole goin' die?" Wilbur panted out the words.

"Looks like it." Lexie leaned against the wall.

"He deserves to burn in hell. That fool would've killed me if it tweren't for you."

"Is that a thank you?"

"Damn sure is."

"Save your energy, Wilbur. You aren't out of the woods yet."

Wilbur rested his head on the filthy sofa arm like an obedient child.

Toby's cough stopped, as did his labored breathing.

It seemed like hours before the helicopter arrived, but it was less than forty minutes. One EMSA person pronounced Toby dead, while the other one wrapped Wilbur's arm.

Turner arrived on a four-wheeler to conduct the follow up investigation. Lexie shut out the horrific scene by focusing on his face. "If you'll handle this, I'll get Flame and head home."

"Can do. This is a bloody mess." Turner's eyes expressed

his concern. "First person you ever killed?"

She nodded.

"You had no choice," Turner assured her, "Wilbur made that clear in his ranting."

"That makes it a little easier, but not much."

Turner waved her out the door. "I'll finish here. Highway patrol is on the way."

Her shoes made scuffmarks in the dirt as she walked into the woods. Lexie's clothes were sprinkled with Toby's blood. A swipe of her tears smeared the red liquid across her cheek. She'd wounded at least a dozen people as a street cop, but none died. She felt empty inside.

Flame's head turned ever so slightly at the sound of her steps. She reached into her saddleback and let him eat hay from her hand. Flame found their way back.

Chapter Forty-Two

After four hours on the plane, Tye's body revolted against the cramped quarters. He attempted to straighten his legs, but it didn't help. He tried to will himself to sleep, or to think about Jamie and Adam. Nothing eased the squashed feeling. Max didn't offer conversation. Walking among the snakes and lizards was sounding better and better. He might try swinging with the monkeys—anything for exercise.

Max pointed, "See that clearing below? That's where we're landing. It's outside a village where we can find you a guide."

"Good, my muscles are stiff." Tye massaged the back of his neck. "I'm ready to chase lizards."

"I noticed your perpetual motion," Max sounded annoyed.

"Movement counteracted the muscle spasms."

"You big guys don't always have the advantage," Max stated.

"I can't argue that."

The plane went downward with a wide smooth swoop. When the plane hit the ground, Tye lunged forward, his head stopped two inches from the window. He noted Max's white knuckles matched his pale face.

"Quite a landing," Tye joked.

"Rough surface, impossible to put it down gently," Max defended.

Tye didn't care what Max thought. It was what it was—a near head-bashing.

The newcomers walked toward half a dozen men. Each

man stared through dark eyes at the out-of-place pair. Tye noticed that two men had right hands strategically located near their hips.

Max greeted them in Spanish, "Hola."

"Hola," Tye repeated.

The men were silent.

Max continued, "There is one hundred dollars for the hombre who will guide this man to the burial plot marked on this paper."

Two men turned and walked away.

A third warned, "Rebels capture and you die."

The fourth man nodded his head in agreement.

Max grumbled, "They're afraid to enter the jungle."

"Not afraid," the fifth man corrected, "I don't die for one hundred dollars American."

The sixth man towered above the others. His words came out in broken English, "I go for four hundred dollars American."

Tye wanted to negotiate, but Max said, "It's a deal." He then reached to shake the man's hand. The guide backed up two steps. Max was left with a hand in the air, which dropped quickly, as if to negate the man's shun.

Tye addressed his guide, "Name?"

A different man answered, "Big Man."

Tye handed Big Man the map. It looked like a note card between his huge hands. One eye followed the directions on the sheet. The other eye peered to the left. His face appeared chiseled out of brown stone. Only three teeth were visible when his lip curled in disgust. Big Man's shaved head revealed a red rash and bloody scratch marks.

Big Man looked like a wild animal that belonged in the

jungle terrain. The guide was at least six inches taller than Tye's height of six-feet-two. Three hundred pounds of muscle was his best bet on weight.

"How many hours will it take us to get in and out?" Tye asked Big Man."

"Veinte," he grunted.

Max retrieved two backpacks from the plane. He tossed the bags toward Tye. "These hold enough supplies for one day. I'll return in twenty-four hours to this spot. If you don't show up within two hours, I'll assume they caught you, or killed you. Either way, I'll head home without you. You sure you want to stay?"

Tye's mouth said, "I'm sure," but his head didn't believe it. "I'll see you tomorrow."

The plane's take-off sent birds flying that Tye had never seen before. He watched as the plane disappeared and wondered if he'd made a mistake. High-tailing it back to civilization with Max was the intelligent choice. *Oh, well, too late now.* At the moment, crunched in a plane was more forbidding than the jungle ahead.

He tossed Big Man a backpack then followed his new partner across the clearing into the jungle. Their heads constantly collided with tree leaves.

Big Man's strides were long. Every few steps, he let out a grunt that indicated a little effort. Tye followed, not worried about lagging behind as long as he heard grunts. Walking eased his muscle cramps. The jungle canopy was so thick that he frequently felt encased in greens and browns. Occasionally, Tye heard the swish of Big Man's machete as he cut down vines that blocked their way. Leaves on the canopy closed off jungle areas, and sunlight was unable to reach the ground. Much of what Tye walked on was bare earth. The insects, birds and frogs offered background noise.

Tye's face crunched in disbelief. He stopped and stared as a line of leaves marched on the path in front of him. With close scrutiny, he saw that underneath each leaf was an ant. The leaves were a hundred times bigger than their transporters, which made it look like each ant carried a sail.

They had walked over two hours when the familiar grunt lapsed. Tye trotted forward fearful he'd lagged too far behind.

"SNAKE."

Big Man's word stopped Tye's movement. He scanned the treetops above his head.

The snake slivered toward Big Man. With one swing of the machete, it became half the snake it once was. Big Man continued his walk and grunt parade without comment.

Tye's clothes stuck like plastic wrap. Humidity was probably ninety percent. Sweat dropped to his eyelids and pooled in his eyelashes. He continually blinked to clear his vision.

Without any warning, the rain poured. Its intensity slowed Tye's forward movement to less than half the speed. He didn't stop. Big Man wasn't the sort who'd let a shower keep him from trudging forward. Tye couldn't hear the familiar grunt over the threshing rain. *Maybe he'll come back for the other two hundred dollars I owe him.*

The rain ended as quickly as it came. Tye did a slow run forward. He searched for Big Man's red flowered shirt, and listened for the life-saving grunt. He finally saw him in the distance. Big Man's pace sped up as soon as he caught sight of Tye.

The rain cooled Tye for a few minutes; but, within half an hour, the jungle turned into nature's sauna. "Big Man," he yelled. "Let's stop for five minutes." He continued moving forward until he saw his guide standing stationary against a tree. Tye sank to the ground and retrieved his water thermos. He drank without stopping. It felt like every ounce of water in his body had evaporated.

Big Man's words shot out, "Come on, girl."

Tye felt his already red face grow ruddier. Any other man and he would've downed him. *Even if he could flatten Big Man, he sure as hell couldn't find his way back without him. This once, he'd let his life take precedence over his pride*

The steady grunt and occasional swish continued for another four hours. Tye didn't ask Big Man to hold up again. The trail opened to a riverbank and Big Man paused to let Tye catch up.

Big Man pointed at the ground, "There."

Tye bent down and explored with his hands. There was a flat stone with the name *Michael Sean Haverty* carved into it.

He searched for the trowels inside his bag and tossed one near his guide's feet. A long and tortuous dig was ahead, and darkness would soon replace daylight. Big Man watched without moving.

"I'd appreciate some help," Tye coaxed, trying to sound friendly.

"No say dig up grave."

"How much will it cost?"

"Two hundred American."

Tye nodded and continued digging.

Big Man dug like an animal making an escape tunnel.

Daylight waned as the two men pulled the casket out of

its hole.

Tye slid his knife under the edge of the wooden lid, then forced it open with a branch. His clothes were soaked from sweat. The heat and exhaustion left him light headed. Big Man backed away from the casket. "Why aren't you helping?"

"No touch dead body—evil."

Tye considered calling him a girl, but decided it wasn't a good idea. Big Man was yards away when Tye opened the coffin.

A skeleton inhabited the box. Based on Sean's story, the body was unexpected. Tye scraped a bone for a DNA sample then studied the remains. He didn't know much about forensics, but he learned that the back branch of a man's jawbone tended to be curved, while a female's was straighter. The female pelvis is formed for childbirth. He had no idea who ended up in Michael's grave, but he knew the skeleton was the remains of a woman. He also knew that Mariah and her dad both lied.

Tye lowered the lid. "Come on, Big Man. Let's put her back to rest."

Big Man moved cautiously toward the coffin.

Tye suppressed the urge to yell, "Boo!" when Big Man came close. He feared the guy would freak. Tye could end up in the hole underneath the casket.

By the time they finished, the lantern was the jungle's only light. Big Man moved toward the trail. Every muscle in Tye's body hurt. Much to his relief, Big Man stopped at a small hut secluded among the trees. He sprawled on the ground and ate food from the backpack. He consumed the filth on his hands with the sandwich.

Tye considered rinsing his hands with thermos water, but decided against it. Water was too valuable to waste on cleanliness. So he, like his partner, consumed some of the days' residue with his supper.

It was a tight fit for the two big men. Tye wasn't sure which of the two smelled worse as he crunched on his side of the hut. Big Man's snoring almost overwhelmed the chorus of insect, bird, and monkey calls outside the hut. The jungle wasn't a peaceful place at night. The racket that entered Tye's head didn't stop him from thinking about the woman he dug up. He wondered how Lexie would respond to this new piece in her puzzle.

Chapter Forty-Three

After two hours sleep and four hours of pain and worry, Tye was exhausted. Big Man waited outside the hut. As soon as he caught sight of Tye, he tromped toward the jungle.

Tye hollered, "Wait up. This girl must pee!" He thought he heard a muffled laugh from Big Man. Tye did his business then returned to the trail. His partner was a few yards in front of him as they moved toward civilization.

He didn't actually see monkeys, but he constantly heard their calls. Tye visually took in all the plants and animals that crossed his path. The mission was finished. He knew who wasn't in the coffin. Now he could appreciate all these sights so foreign to a country boy.

Three hours into their trek, he veered off the path to take care of nature's call. Why Big Man didn't have any elimination needs was beyond Tye. He crouched and pondered which of the various vegetation leaves he should use to wipe his butt.

A loud angry voice sucked the air out of Tye's lungs. He breathed in with all his might to put some oxygen back into his body. He pulled up his jeans then slumped back down. He stayed off the path as he crawled forward. Soon he saw Big Man on his belly. His hands tied behind him. A small man stood over him yelling loudly in Spanish. A long leather whip was in the captor's hand. He hit Big Man between loud Spanish ravings. Three smiling men watched as the whip met its' target.

Big Man was a huge lump on the ground. *Is he dead? No, there's foot movement. These must be the rebels Max warned me about.* Max's words reverberated in Tye's brain: 'Men who'd kill you, or hold you prisoner for the rest of your life.' He could easily get past them and make his way back to the airplane. Big Man wouldn't risk his life if things were reversed.

One of the men put a rope around Big Man's neck and jerked him up. A huge dog on a leash was led deeper into the jungle. The others pointed their guns at Big Man's head.

Tye kept his distance as he followed. After a few minutes, they stopped and tied Big Man to a tree. They sat on a patch of jungle floor and ate lunch, constantly interrupting each other in Spanish.

Tye rounded the tree, and loosened the rope around Big Man's neck. The knot was so tight that he used his knife. Big Man followed Tye back through the underbrush then he took the lead.

The grunt was gone now. The constant thump of their feet against the jungle's dirt floor, and the insects in the distance, were the only sounds. They ran at least twenty minutes before Big Man slowed his pace.

Tye wondered what the rebels thought when they went to get their prisoner. He hoped the prospect of ghosts in the jungle kept them awake all night.

A rapid walk continued the journey. Big Man offered no thanks to the 'girl' who saved his life.

Tye spotted Max drinking a beer beside his plane. "Am I late?"

"You had fifteen minutes before I left you here to rot."

"The old timers used to say, 'all's well that ends well.' I'm here with time to spare and I'm still alive. I've had a good day." Tye pulled four hundred dollars out of his wallet then headed toward Big Man. The two met halfway. Tye reached four bills toward him.

"No want," Big Man crushed the previously paid bills in with the four that were in Tye's hand.

"You earned this money," Tye insisted.

"No, for my Amigo."

"Amigo, yes!" Tye slapped Big Man's back as he pushed money in his pocket.

"No girl," Big Man smiled, showing his three teeth.

"Damn right," Tye laughed.

"Gracias, Amigo!" Big Man hollered as Tye lifted himself into the plane.

"What's that about?" Max questioned after the plane was airborne.

"Long story," Tye yawned.

Within five minutes, exhaustion took over and he slept all the way to Panama.

Chapter Forty-Four

As Lexie sat at her kitchen table on Friday morning, she lamented on how slow Wednesday and Thursday passed. She likened it to waiting for a monster to show up. On constant alert every second of every day sapped her energy. Apprehensive thoughts of the upcoming reunion resulted in headaches and nausea. Her only solace being that Tye returned home with valuable information and jungle stories to tell anyone who listened.

I should've quit after Abbey's death. "No, I can do this. I *will* get Abbey's killer." Her self-reprimand maneuvered her brain from self-doubt into action. She stood abruptly, fastened her gun holster, and hand-swiped her wrinkled uniform shirt. Nothing but an iron would improve her appearance. She didn't have the time or the will to perform a mundane task.

A saying kept going through her head as she drove into town, 'fake it to make it.'

The men arrived before her. She pretended confidence as she stood in front of them. "The school gymnasium was checked for bombs," Lexie reported. "The gym dedication takes place tonight. Saturday afternoon there's a picnic at the park."

"I'm more worried about the park than the gym," Tye declared, "it's a much bigger area to cover."

Lexie agreed. "Based on history, the murderer likes killing outdoors. Turner will guard Beth, Loretta and Jamie this afternoon while they finish last minute dedication preparations at Loretta's house."

"Stupid for them to be at the same place," Clay countered.

"We don't have enough manpower to protect them separately all day." Lexie paused, "Anyway, Loretta said they couldn't pull off the dedication ceremony without prep time today."

"I'm heading that way right now," Turner informed, "I'll get stationed before Jamie and Beth show-up."

"It's time for all of us to take our posts. Thanks for helping, and be careful out there."

Lexie drove to the gym. Every door was locked and highway patrolmen stood guard at every entry.

"Your captain told me that he assigned each of you to one of the possible murder victims. Correct?"

"Yes," a man responded. He looked like a seventeen-year-old. "We'll guard them with our lives."

Lexie shook her head. This assignment required experience, not a wild-eyed rookie. She drove to Main Street and parked at the fork where most traffic came into town. Around noon, the early birds arrived. The local motel was filled, according to the owner. Many of the returnees had relatives in Diffee with whom they stayed. A few lodged in Tulsa.

Lexie retrieved her phone from the passenger seat. "Loretta, is everything okay there?"

"I suppose it is. Beth left decorations until the last minute. Hardly time left to get ready."

"Is Officer Turner staying close?"

"He makes me nervous the way he stalks about," Loretta whined like a spoiled child, "I'm tired of him bringing dirt in on his big shoes. I'd send him back to you, but my husband is in town setting up the stage for the presentation."

"I'll arrest you for hampering an investigation if you give him a hard time," Lexie retorted.

Loretta was taken aback. "You sound serious."

"Never more so. Have you heard anything from Mariah?"

"Five minutes ago she phoned, and asked to spend the night here. Donovan can't come, and she's nervous about staying alone tonight."

"If you hear or see anything the least bit suspicious, tell Turner."

"Yes, I will." Loretta sounded cooperative for once.

"Let me talk to Turner."

"It's for you," Lexie heard Loretta say in the background.

"Turner."

"It's Lexie. Search their cars before they leave, then follow them into town. When you get to the gym, check in with me, then go home and sleep."

"I don't mind staying on duty."

"I appreciate that, but you must stay alert at the picnic tomorrow." Lexie startled when someone rapped on her back window.

"Special delivery from OSBI," the man said loudly, trying to compensate for the closed windows.

She rolled down the window and reached for the parcel. "Thanks. Just what I wanted."

Lexie opened the package and found Michael's prints from Interpol. She drove back to her office, pulled the print from the lip gloss, and put it between those of the Haverty siblings. Without reading the report, she saw that Michael's prints clearly matched those from the crime scene. Now her job was easier. She was looking for a tall man with a toupee.

The photo she had of him was twenty years old.

She phoned Bryce at OSBI. "Can someone age a photograph for me? It's my killer."

"Get it to me."

"I'm on my way."

"Delia, I'll be back ASAP. Tell Tye I'll bring a sketch of the murderer to the gym."

Delia's mouth flew open. "Who is it?"

"It's a long story that'll wait until later." Lexie's steps reached the door as her remark ended.

Her mind didn't drift from the murder case during her drive to Tulsa. Lexie approached the OSBI front desk, "Where's Bryce?"

"Who are you?" the woman responded.

"The Diffee Sheriff. He's expecting me."

The woman motioned toward a door.

Bryce was a wild-haired brunette. She handed him the photo.

He opened the envelope, "You got here fast."

Her voice shook, "I'm expecting that guy to show up in my county and kill four women."

"That's good reason to hurry. I'll give this to Webber. Leave your cell number and I'll phone when he's finished."

"I appreciate it."

She found a restaurant nearby. The coffee she ordered tasted foul. Brown trim on the lettuce and mushy tomatoes didn't make for an appetizing salad. She left the lousy food on the table and headed toward the exit.

"You didn't pay," the manager yelped as he followed her across the parking lot. "Cops don't get free meals here."

Lexie fired back, "I should arrest you for serving that

garbage. I had one bite and one swallow. The dollar I owe is on the table."

"BULLSHIT!"

Lexie drove back to the OSBI building. She parked in the lot to await her call. The warm breeze lulled her to sleep.

"Hey, are you okay?" The words intermingled with the tapping on her window.

"Yes, I'm okay. Big case—no sleep."

"I know the feeling. Are you Sheriff Wolfe?"

"That's me."

"I'm Webber. Your sketch is ready."

"Thanks so much," Lexie exited the cruiser.

She signed out the drawing from Bryce. "I appreciate this, not to mention the extra copies."

"Go get'em, Sheriff!"

She drove too fast, but she was anxious to get the flyers distributed. It was close to 4 p.m. and she had to match faces to Webber's drawing. She'd feel jubilant if they caught the murderer before the celebration.

Her mind mulled over why Michael killed the women. The only thing that fit was what Tye thought: Mariah told Michael something that provoked him. The logical reason was that twenty years ago, in a drunken state, Mariah told her friends that her murdering brother was alive. If she recently confessed to him that she told his secret, it would explain why he killed the women.

Tye approached when she entered the gym. "What's this about a murderer's photo?"

She handed him half the pictures.

They dispersed the drawings to men at various posts in the gym. Now it was time to wait, worry, and watch.

Chapter Forty-Five

Mariah didn't have any trouble finding Loretta's pompous two-story house. She had visited when the house belonged to Loretta's grandma. The constant curves and hilly terrain made for a strenuous drive. The colonial house sat on top of a hill with tall pines strategically located so as not to hamper the view. The woods were stripped around her house to accommodate the pines. Tall trees that descended down the hill surrounded the frame of pines.

A highway patrol car was parked a hundred yards or so from the house. When Mariah was in sight of the vehicle, she turned, drove past the house, and backed into a cluster of trees.

"What's your business?" Turner called.

Mariah rolled down her window. "Came to help my friends. I assume you know about the dedication tonight."

"Sure do," Turner answered.

"I'm Mariah Toleson."

"I know who you are. Didn't recognize you at first 'cause of the sun. I can't wait to tell my wife I saw the next First Lady. You go right on in!"

"May I park here? I feel safer coming and going near you."

"Sure, good idea," Turner saluted.

The doorbell tune was an old southern song—the name eluded Mariah.

Loretta looked confused when she opened the door. "I wasn't expecting to see you until the dedication."

"I got in early. Thought I'd be of assistance."

"Come in, Beth and Jamie are in the family room writing memorials for our dead teammates."

Beth looked up, "Mariah Rose..."

Jamie interrupted, "It's been a long time. As Loretta told me, 'Put your ass on a chair and get busy.'"

"I wasn't talking about Mariah. It was meant for you two, who put this off until the last possible minute," Loretta argued.

Jamie shot back, "I kept thinking you or I would get murdered then I wouldn't have to work with you."

Beth chimed in, "Time doesn't change anything, Mariah. They still have the 'hate-barely tolerate each other' relationship from twenty years ago."

Mariah sat down at the table. "I'll make more tissue paper flowers."

"We have enough." Loretta shoved a pen and paper towards her. "Write and present Terri's memorial."

Mariah pushed the paper back. "Best I'm not part of the program. That would center attention on me instead of our dead friends."

Beth changed the subject. "Do you think about how it will feel if you become first lady?"

Mariah sighed, "A dream come true."

"We'll visit you at the White house," Loretta stated.

"I don't think that's a good idea."

The raw nerve Mariah hit was evident in Loretta's stinging tone. "Now you're too high and mighty for us? Before, you promised us anything we wanted to keep our mouths shut, but now you don't want us around?"

"I never told anyone and I never will," Beth blurted.

"Mariah, when you swirled around that night with your

penis bobbing—I thought Loretta was going to choke. First time she was ever left speechless." Jamie didn't suppress the cackle that rose from her throat.

"A First Lady with a penis. That's news worthy." Sarcasm dripped from Loretta's words.

"There's no penis now. I'm a better woman than any of you." Mariah's angry gaze shot to Jamie, then Loretta.

Loretta continued her attack. "You didn't mind talking about my abortion, so why shouldn't I tell about you?"

"You didn't tell I was male, because you would've lost your precious championship because there was a boy on your team." Mariah leaped from her chair knocking it to the floor. She ran into the kitchen. The door swung back and forth behind her.

"You two are cruel."

Mariah heard Beth's reprimand, then the kitchen door opened. Mariah sat on the top basement step. Her hands covered her face.

Beth touched her shoulder. "They'll never tell your secret."

Mariah rose from the step. With one strong tug, she flung Beth down the stairs. She smashed into the cement floor below. Mariah watched for movement, but none came.

"Help! Help! Oh my God!" Mariah screamed.

The kitchen door slammed repetitively against the wall when Jamie ran through.

"She tripped on the steps," Mariah moaned. "I'll phone an ambulance."

Mariah stepped aside as they ran down the steps, and then she closed and locked the door behind them. They gave no sounds that indicated they were trapped like animals.

Mariah jogged out of the house and toward Turner.

"Can I help you?" Turner yelled.

Mariah's feet barely touched the ground as she ran behind the garden shed.

Turner followed, "What do you want?"

She aimed the gun directly at Turner's chest. "I wanted you dead." Mariah told the officer lying in the dirt."

She pulled the gas can out of her car trunk and jogged to the kitchen. Intermittently, she heard Jamie and Loretta's screams. The fools thought they were locked in by accident.

Spilling the gas over the kitchen floor, she made a line to the living room then forked out to both the front and back doors. Mariah visualized the old wood floor burning above their heads, and an avalanche of fire and rubble consuming all of them. Her secret would die with them.

Chapter Forty-Six

Lexie approached Tye in a panic. "Where are they? It's six o'clock. They should be here."

"Don't get spooked, Loretta probably chipped a fingernail."

Her head throbbed as she listened to Turner's phone buzz and buzz. It reminded her of the night Tye called to report Abbey's death. She hung up, then her phone rang.

Tye sounded positive, "That's Turner."

"Sheriff Wolfe, this is Bryce. Didn't you say that Mariah Haverty and Mariah Toleson are the same person?"

"Yes." Her hand tightened on the phone.

"Then the Interpol prints were marked wrong. Mariah's recent prints didn't match the ones from Interpol. You should also know that the DNA from the gravesite was a family member of Sean and Mariah Haverty.

"Okay." Lexie ended the conversation as her brain absorbed the shock. "Tye, phone Clay. Tell him to meet me at the bottom of Loretta's hill in twenty minutes. Ask the chief to make contact with Turner. You're in charge here. Catch the murderer."

"Will do," Tye called as she ran out the door.

Lexie was at her office within five minutes. She pulled the prints from the file. Mariah Toleson and Mariah Haverty's prints didn't match. Then she pulled Michael's prints. They were identical to Mariah Haverty's recent prints. *Bryce was right. They screwed up my case. They mismarked the prints of the siblings.*

Lexie ran to her patrol car. She pushed in Loretta's

number as she drove. The incessant buzzing continued until the machine requested a message. Lexie pushed redial time after time. When she reached the bottom of Loretta's hill, she signaled Clay to follow. The smell of smoke invaded her nostrils. *Not a fire on top of all this*! She sped up the winding road. The trees camouflaged her view as she searched visually for the source of the smoke. When the pine trees became visible, so did the flames firing red and yellow spirals from the lower level house windows.

"CLAY!" She hollered as she ran toward the house. "Phone the fire department and ambulance."

"Do you want Tye here?"

"No, it may be a trick." Lexie ran into the smoke. The front door was on fire. She sped to the rear, but it, too, was engulfed in flames.

"Help me! Help me!" a female voice screamed.

Lexie's arms circled Mariah and pulled her to standing. "Was anyone else in the house?"

Mariah hollered words into the night. "My friends are dead!"

Lexie's heart pounded, "Who's dead?"

"Beth, Loretta, and Jamie."

"I'll get them!" Lexie shouted above the fire.

Mariah grasped her arm. "NO, you'll die too."

"Go to Clay," Lexie ordered. Mariah kept her grip. Lexie clenched Mariah's hand and pried it from her wrist releasing the hold.

"Clay, don't let her out of your sight."

Lexie decided to enter through the basement and make her way to the first floor. Dirt flew as her hands cleared the basement window. The glass crashed easily with the weight of her gun handle. She stared at solid wood four inches from the window.

"Is anyone in there?" she yelled.

"We're here," a hoarse voice answered.

"What's in front of me?"

"An old cabinet," A long cough interrupted Jamie's words.

"You three help me pull it down."

Loretta's voice boomed, "Beth is hurt bad!"

"Get her out of the way," Lexie ordered. "When I say three, you two pull down from the sides, while I push. One-two-three."

The cabinet crashed. Lexie saw them below.

"You two push Beth up."

"I can't. The window's too high!" Loretta cried out on the verge of hysteria. "She's already dying. If I don't get out of here, I'll die, too."

Loretta stood on the mangled cabinet. Jamie gave her a boost with her cradled hands. Loretta grabbed Lexie's hands and walked up the wall. When she reached the top, Lexie pulled her out the window.

"Jamie, get out right now." Lexie ordered.

"I won't leave Beth. She's alive."

Lexie heard Loretta scream above the fire's roar. She turned as Loretta ran straight toward Mariah.

"You tried to kill us, you bastard!"

Mariah stepped to the side and Loretta crashed to the ground. Mariah ran into the woods.

"Go get her! "Lexie yelled.

Clay ran into the woods as Turner's patrol car sped out of the thicket. Mariah swerved to avoid a fire truck. Clay ran to his car and chased her down the winding road.

Chapter Forty-Seven

Sweat trickled from every pore of Mariah's body. The patrol car twisted with each bump and hollow in the curved road. At times the rear end of the car hung in the air as she pushed the gas to the floor. At ninety mph, the patrol car squealed in protest.

Fire trucks passed her. The sirens vibrated in her head and lightening pains shot into her temple. Truck after truck, patrol car after patrol car, and three ambulances shot rocks in the air around her as they sped by. They hurried to their official destination, paying no attention to the murderer they passed. Her mouth parted, which allowed a prickly laugh to escape.

Her rearview mirror caught the reflection of a cloud of dust descending with rapid speed. The particles swirled then ballooned toward the sky. The dust from the two vehicles merged. Her body lunged forward as the impact of the other car bumper sent her car flying forward. Her foot smashed the gas pedal as her aggressor increased his speed. Death was better than life in prison. Her hands froze on the steering wheel. Her body and shoulder found the strength to force Turner's vehicle off the road, and down the side of the giant hill.

The trees allowed only inches to squeeze through on either side. A boulder loomed ahead. She turned the wheel to the right, and missed hitting the rock head on, but scraped the driver's side, which sent a piercing squeal into the air. The trees blurred together as the car shot ever downward. The rocky ledge and certain death came closer and closer.

Mariah's body deteriorated into a trembling mass. Her hands released the wheel as she pushed herself to the passenger side. The door handle responded to her frantic squeeze, and she fell out the door. Fallen branches stabbed her back, and rocks punctured her arms and legs. Her roll continued until her body wrapped around a tree. Her face slapped the exposed roots.

The earth shook beneath her, and the sky became a panorama of fire. Her funeral pyre exploded without her.

Her body lay still. Her brain uncertain if she'd ever move again. Long and short pains assaulted her body. Blood popped out of small indentions and oozed out of larger ones. The curve of her body released the tree trunk and she lay on her back. She wiggled her fingers and toes, then turned her head in a 'no' motion. She smoothed the dirt from her face. Soothing her riddled hip with a gentle sweeping movement, she moved her hands to feel her knees and elbows, then sat up with a great deal of pain. She wondered what was taking her pursuer so long to arrive. Wrapping her arms around the tree, she pulled herself up then rested her forehead on the bark before trying her legs. They worked—one sore, the other one throbbed in unison with the hip that impacted the ground.

The sound of running steps trickled into her aching head. The blonde curly hair of a young man in uniform appeared above her as she sank back to the ground. He looked puzzled.

"Come to confirm my death?" Mariah squeezed the words out of her tortured body.

He stuttered the affirmative.

"I'll make you rich if you save me."

His blue eyes widened, his tongue apparently tied.

"You can have all the girls and booze you want and burn that stupid uniform."

"They'd catch me."

"Look at the fire and smoke in the valley. They'll all think I died in the car crash. You're a hero who chased me to my death."

Clay stared at her through bloodshot eyes.

"Get me to town. Let me take your vehicle. I'll leave it at the Tulsa Airport."

"I got to get back to the fire."

"It won't take long. Drive me to town. I'll clean up at your place. You'll be a wealthy man."

"How much?"

"$100,000.00"

Blonde curls rippled with his shaking head, "Not enough."

"All right, $250,000.00. I don't have time for negotiation. I've got to get out of here."

"How do I get my money?"

"You've got the upper hand. If I don't pay, you can talk. I'll send you the money when I get to Switzerland. Don't start flaunting it or it'll cause suspicion."

"I'm not stupid."

The climb to the road was slow and painful, but her new accomplice served as an adequate crutch, as well as her savior.

Chapter Forty-Eight

"Help me!" Lexie yelled.

"I'll go down," one fireman offered.

"You're too big. I'll go."

An explosion sent spikes of fire skyward. Lexie looked down the hill in horror. "Please, God, not Clay."

She returned to her task. "You two guys ease me into the basement."

Her stomach scraped against the fragmented glass and dirt as they lowered her down onto the cabinet debris.

She put the harness on Beth's body. "Okay guys, pull her up easy."

Jamie and Lexie supported Beth's lower body as the men pulled her through the opening.

Lexie heard the chief yell for the EMSA people. She helped Jamie put on the rescue harness. "Hold onto the rope. The men will pull you," Lexie encouraged.

Jamie grabbed the rope. Burned fragments from the kitchen fell, hit the basement floor and swirled around Lexie as she pushed Jamie toward the firemen.

A few minutes later, the harness was lowered to Lexie and she walked up the wall. Strong arms pulled her exhausted body out the window.

The EMSA team was working on Beth when Lexie and Jamie got to the ambulances.

"Get in there and lie down," Lexie instructed.

Jamie went without argument.

"Better get in the other ambulance," the chief advised.

"I'm okay," she muttered.

The siren from Beth's ambulance pierced through the darkness as it headed toward the hospital. Jamie's soon followed.

A shaky voice called from behind her, "Lexie!"

"Clay!" Her arms wrapped around his trembling body. "I was afraid you crashed."

"Mariah is dead." His voice was subdued. "Looked like a ball of fire. There was nothing left."

Lexie heard her name called then saw Red come toward her with long strides. He enveloped her in his arms as her legs buckled. He picked her up in one motion and carried her to a third ambulance.

The oxygen allowed calmness. She no longer had to work so hard to breathe. The woman cleaned the glass cuts on her hands, arms, and midriff. Each time her eyes opened, Red was beside her, so she allowed them to stay closed. He kept watch.

Chapter Forty-Nine

"Wake up, Lexie," the nurse ordered. "It's time for your medicine."

Lexie wrinkled her forehead in an attempt to keep her eyes open, but they closed anyway.

"Come on, Sis. You crawled through fire, surely you can open your eyes."

Lexie forced her puffy eyes open. She looked at her brother. "Don't you have something better to do than harass hospital patients?"

"My boss is off so I played hooky."

Lexie's tone turned serious. "What happened with the fires?"

"Firemen worked most of the night. That recent rain helped. They called in the volunteer fire departments from three surrounding counties. There are still a few men on site, making sure it doesn't start up again."

"How about the area where Mariah's car caught fire?"

"Her car was a burned out shell. What a terrible way to die!"

"In her case, it was the appropriate way," Lexie spouted vehemently, "since that was how she planned to kill her former teammates."

"True. Anyway, the creek stopped the fire on one side and the firemen got it under control. It was the house that took the work. Fire chief said that it saved the women's lives that Mariah locked them in the basement. The cement floor and walls slowed down the burn. If she'd locked them in any other place in the house, they'd never have survived."

"Have you talked to Sean?"

"No. That's my next stop, but I wanted to discuss it first," Tye answered.

"He withheld evidence. Charge him and let the judge decide his fate," Lexie directed.

"Lock him up?"

"Not yet, he won't go anywhere but his front porch. Ask him his story. I can't separate the truth from the lies about his children. Maybe he'll talk since Mariah is dead."

"Loretta didn't shut up last night," Tye grimaced. "Adam interviewed her for over an hour and she spilled her guts, with numerous cuss words intermingled."

"I'd like to read that."

"As it happens, I brought the paper. Wanted you to read Mariah's story, not to mention Adam's accolades to Sheriff Lexie.

"Thanks, big brother. I guess you're useful even when you're playing hooky."

Tye ruffled her hair. "I'll interview Sean and you get some rest. See you tonight."

Lexie viewed the front page. Two-inch headlines monopolized the page: POLITICIAN'S WIFE DIES IN FIREY CRASH and SHERIFF WOLFE SAVES THREE LIVES introduced separate stories.

Her eyes immediately went to Mariah's story:

Mariah Haverty Toleson is implicated in the murders of four women, including Abbey King, wife of local resident Gary King. Toleson attempted to murder three Diffee residents Friday night by locking them in a basement and setting the house on fire.

Loretta Wells of Diffee unfolded a twenty-year-old saga

after her near-death experience yesterday. Wells' story explained why Toleson committed a series of murders to cover up her past.

Their story began near the Illinois River the day after the team won the state Girl's Basketball Championship. The eight: Heather (Hobart) Blanchard, Loretta (Baldwin) Wells, Terri (Davidson) Womack, Jamie Evans, Abbey (Lansing) King, Tina (Morris) Smith, Beth (Ross) Flanders, and Toleson were a source of pride for the people of the small town of Diffee, Oklahoma.

Resident Ruben Thomas described the girls' impact on the town. "Town closed down every Friday night so we could watch the girls play. They were great! Their senior season was flawless—not one loss, not even close."

It was after the season ended, during a celebration campout at the lake, that the young women followed Mariah into the woods to play a trick on her. The joke ended abruptly when the team members saw a shocking sight—Mariah had a penis.

"Our season and our reputations would've been destroyed if anyone found out a male played on our team. We swore never to tell Mariah's secret," Loretta confessed in tears.

According to Loretta, Mariah was obsessed at the prospect of becoming First Lady. Wells believed this provoked the series of murders. Mariah's plot was to end last night when she trapped Beth, Jamie, and Loretta in a burning house. The detective work of Sheriff Lexie Wolfe prevented the deaths. Wolfe accumulated evidence and figured out who the killer was in time to rescue Beth, Loretta, and Jamie from their fiery deaths planned by Mariah Toleson.

Beth Flanders and Sheriff Wolfe are recovering at the county hospital. Jamie and Loretta were examined at the hospital last night and released.

"Terri Womack's husband, Ronald, who was charged with her death, will be released after a court appearance to drop the charges," Lasell Detective Stan Johnson reported.

Wade Cartwright, spokesman for Donovan Toleson, reported that Mr. Toleson isn't making a statement regarding the tragic death of his wife, or the allegations of murder and attempted murder.

Reading the long story made Lexie's body feel like she'd run for miles. Her eyelids shut, and the paper dropped to her chest.

Chapter Fifty

Tye approached Sean's porch. He hated confronting the old guy. Whatever he did, it was to protect his kids, not because he was a criminal. Getting Lexie to cut Sean some slack wasn't going to happen. Hopefully, the judge had more empathy than his sister.

The old man wasn't seated on the swing. Tye's gaze darted from the porch across the surrounding area. He called out, "Sean?"

The front door was ajar. He peered through the opening into the dark living room. "Sean, are you okay?"

Wood on wood creaked somewhere in the room. It took a few seconds before Tye's eyes adjusted to the darkness. Finally, pinpointing the location of the sound, he saw Sean rocking back and forth in an old chair. Every few seconds the chair squealed as if in pain from contact with the wooden floor.

Sean's eyes didn't divert from the photo in his hands. Age crevices in his face caught the escaping tears.

Tye sat down at the end of the sofa closest to Sean's rocking chair. The steady rock and squeal was the only communication in the room.

Tye didn't know what to say, and even if he knew, this didn't seem the time. He sat, waiting silently for the next squeal from the chair. After twenty minutes, the squeal stopped and Sean placed the photo in Tye's hand.

"This was my family—my wife Rose, my son Michael, and my daughter Mariah. They're all gone now." He grabbed the photo back from Tye and continued, "I'm sorry Bud killed those women. I should've had him locked up after he drowned Mariah. I couldn't do it. He was my son, and the only family I had left."

Sean pulled the photo to his chest. The rock and squeal returned. "So sorry, so sorry everyone died."

"Tell me about Mariah." Although Tye said the words softly, they sounded intrusive in Sean's self-made tomb.

"A beautiful girl. She sang like an angel. There were days when the thought of her smile and giggles were what kept me sane," Sean said tenderly.

"How did she die?"

The squeal and rock stopped. Sean's voice boomed, "He killed her! I know he did!"

"Did you see it?"

"No. Michael swore it was an accidental drowning. She swam like a fish—under the water, on top of the water, and diving into the water. He lied."

"Why did he lie?" Tye questioned in a gentle tone.

Agitation crept into Sean's demeanor. "He wanted to be Mariah Rose so he killed her. I let him become her, because he was so sad, so sad."

"I don't understand how he became her."

"Fool!" Sean yelled. "It was easy." His voice went monotone, "Nobody cared about us in Bogotá. Who we were, or what we did, didn't matter. I told them Michael drowned. I cut Mariah's hair short, dressed her in his clothes, nailed her in a wood coffin and buried her. Michael's name was on the tombstone. It's as if she never was. I did that to my precious girl."

"Then what happened?"

"I retired from the Embassy. My commanding officer

was glad to sign the paperwork. He thought I was crazy after losing my wife and child. Looking back, he was probably right. Of course, he didn't know the half of it."

Sean let out a moan, then continued, "I took Michael to Switzerland as Mariah. The hormone treatments started there. Right before his senior year, we moved to Diffee to live in this old house that my folks left me. I was about broke. The doctor refused to do the sex reassignment surgery until after Michael spent a year as a female. Returning to Diffee was the perfect solution. It was a cheap place to live and no one had ever met my children."

"The girls saw his penis that night by the lake?" Tye asked.

"Yes, but I thought it was okay because none of them wanted the championship taken away from them. Jamie and Loretta had their own secrets. Bud could hold that over their heads if they threatened to tell his. Everything was fine until Bud's husband became a bigwig."

"You called her Bud?"

"Yes, I couldn't bear to call him Mariah. He became Mariah Rose, but I called him Bud. Rosebud was my wife's nickname. So I called him Bud and told him it was after his mother."

"What brought on all the killing?"

"Bud became obsessed with becoming First Lady. As Donovan was mentioned more and more frequently as a possible nominee, Bud became paranoid about the others telling his secret."

"Sounds like you knew he killed those women."

"I didn't have proof, only fear."

"Why did you lie about Mariah's brother still being

alive?" Tye questioned.

"If you thought her murdering brother was alive, then you'd have a logical suspect and you'd leave Bud alone."

"You made up that story to save Bud?"

"Yes. I gave you a different murderer. I sent you looking for a person who no longer existed."

"Sean, you're an accessory to murder."

"It doesn't matter. There's nothing left. Are you taking me to jail?"

"Not now—stay home and I'll return later to ask more questions."

The steady rock and squeal resumed.

Tye squinted his eyes as he adjusted to the brightness of the outside world. He organized his thoughts. First, he'd phone Clay and have him sit with Sean. Second, he'd go to Judge Simpson to get a court order for a psychological evaluation of Sean. Third, he'd transport Sean to his new accommodations.

Chapter Fifty-One

Mariah's eyes scanned every face she passed as she went toward the elevator at the Tulsa hotel. No one would look for her, unless Curly Boy got a surge of conscience.

She put her laptop on the desk when she entered the room. A few minutes later, she purchased tickets from Tulsa to New York to Switzerland.

The soap stung the bloody pocks on her body and she quickly sprayed the warm shower water to lessen the sting. Twice the recommended pain medication did nothing to relieve her misery. No doctor visit until she was out of the country.

Mariah knew how close she came to death. At the very least, law enforcement should knock down her door. At the most, the fiery inferno should've taken her life. She was invincible—risen from the ashes. Her sole life goal was the pursuit of the ultimate terror and sorrow for Sheriff Lexie Wolfe. The woman who destroyed Mariah's future will be tortured then a stake hammered through her heart.

She packed her bag and straightened the wig. The lipstick, powder, and all things feminine were trashed. She was the man in the mirror.

He left Clay's car in the airport lot. This, the first leg of his journey, would end in a couple of days in his chateau in Switzerland—a free man.

Mariah died a second death and this time she'd remain dead. Bud had plenty of time to rest, recover, and plan before he returned to America in a year or two as a new woman.

Chapter Fifty-Two

The flames surrounded Lexie—red and yellow flares of hotness. Gray smoke engulfed her body. It crept up her nose: choke, choke, choke, cough, cough, cough. The flares of fire were taller than she. They met and formed an arch above her head.

Mariah stood in the distance wearing Turner's hat and badge. She yelled, "Burn, Sheriff, burn!"

"No, no, no!" Lexie screamed. The blanket flew from her body and her eyes rounded in terror. Her deep cough shot pains through her heaving chest.

"It's a nightmare." The woman lowered Lexie back to the pillow. "You're safe here."

Lexie took her outstretched hand in both of hers. The nurse petted her hair. "It's okay now. It's over. The fire is over."

Releasing her hold, Lexie sat up on the bed. "I'm sorry. It was so real."

"Don't be sorry, Sheriff. Yesterday was a hell of a day. I mean H-E-L-L in all caps."

"That it was," Lexie agreed.

"I forgot. You have a visitor. Adam from the paper is here to interview you. I'll run him off if you're not up to it."

"Have him wait ten minutes, then come in. May I have some water?"

"Of course and I'll give him the message." The nurse handed Lexie water to sip.

Ten minutes to the minute, or probably to the second,

Adam arrived at the door. "Is it okay if I come in?"

"Of course, Adam."

"I see you have the paper."

"Yes, I read your story before I fell asleep. I woke up from a bad dream and scattered it on the floor."

Adam bent down and folded the sheets. "Do you like the story?"

"I think that one day you'll leave Diffee and become a big time reporter. It was great! I especially appreciated your kindness toward me. Maybe the folks who want to lynch me will reconsider."

"My story was picked up all over the United States and even in some foreign countries." He said the words in rapid succession.

"You did a great job, Adam. I'm proud of you."

"May I take a photo?"

"Generally the answer is 'no.' However, I'll agree to a photo this time. Let me warn you—it will probably be the last time."

He pulled his camera out of a bag, "Thanks."

Lexie smoothed her hair, then pulled the sheet up to her armpits. Adam suggested that she pretend to read the paper, she cooperated.

A blonde nurse entered, "Adam, get downstairs. They brought your grandpa into the emergency room."

Adam's voice was barely audible, "What's wrong with him?"

The nurse spoke to his back as he ran out the door. "It's his heart."

"Are Adam's mom and dad downstairs?" Lexie questioned.

"No, his folks are dead," the nurse replied. "He and his grandpa are my neighbors. He's all the family the boy has as far as I know."

"Poor kid."

"Time for medicine rounds. I'll check on you in a few minutes."

Lexie grinned, "I know you have to wait until I'm asleep so you can wake me."

She winked, "It's people like you who give us nurses bad reputations."

Lexie's cell phone rang its familiar tune. "Hello, Bro, I'm doing fine. I'd like to escape this place and sleep. Our friendly town reporter, Adam, was in my room getting a story when a nurse came and got him. His grandpa was in the emergency room with a heart problem. Kid turned white as a ghost. Tye, are you still there? I can't hear you? She listened for a response then continued, "Don't come up tonight. I'm doing fine."

His next words confused her. "Why are you coming to the hospital to sit with Adam?" The phone clicked and the connection went dead. *That's strange.*

She considered turning on the television, but her body decided on an alternative. The air conditioner lulled her back to sleep. The dream that followed was of a redheaded man who kept kissing her again, and again, and again…

Chapter Fifty-Three

Tye wasn't sure of why he hurried to the hospital. The emergency room was empty except for a boy in a ball uniform holding his right arm. His mother was yelling about the evils of baseball to a man who must have been the kid's father.

Tye stopped the first nurse he saw. "Where's Dr. Carr?"

"On the third floor in surgery. There's a family waiting room on that floor."

"Thanks." Tye trotted to the elevator.

Adam was looking out the window when Tye walked in. "How's your grandpa?"

Adam turned. "Not good. His heartbeat went down to thirty and the doc's putting in a pacemaker. Told me not to get my hopes up."

"I'm sorry to hear that." Tye sat on the leather sofa near the window.

"You here visiting your sister? She let me take her photo for the newspaper."

"She's the one who told me your grandpa was taken to the emergency room. Did he talk to you?"

Adam's eyes clouded. "For a minute, but he wasn't making any sense."

"How's that?"

"He said 'sorry,' then something about finding my brother. I don't have a brother."

Tye sat silently, unsure of what to say. He made a promise, but Carr tried to tell Adam the truth.

Tye took a deep breath. "Your grandpa was sorry because

he never told you that you were adopted at birth by his daughter and her husband. You were the biological son of two teenagers. The girl's father arranged for the adoption. The boy never knew about you until recently." Tye knew the onrush of information overwhelmed the boy.

Adam's face reflected the emotional turbulence inside. "Please leave me alone." He dropped into a chair beside the window.

Tye slowly rose from the sofa. "I'll be in Lexie's room if you want to talk."

Adam's voice stopped him as he reached the door. "I have a brother?"

"Yes," Tye answered, "a twin brother."

"Where is he?"

"I don't know. You two were separated at birth."

Adam turned his chair toward the window, shutting out Tye and the rest of the world.

Tye took the stairs to Lexie's room. Sleeping soundly, she didn't stir when he entered. He sat in the chair beside her bed, he was relieved that he didn't have to make conversation.

A few minutes passed before Adam arrived in the room. The door banged against the wall with the strength of his entry.

Lexie startled from sleep. "What are you people doing here? Watching me sleep?"

Adam stuttered, "How do you know so much about me?"

Tye answered calmly, "I'm your father."

Lexie's mouth gaped, "What?"

"Who is my mother?"

"Jamie Evans is your mother. She doesn't know that I

found one of our sons."

"She gave us away?"

"Jamie was a scared teenager who followed her dad's orders."

Adam's voice resonated with unbelief, "You didn't know about me?"

"No. Your grandpa admitted it when I was at his place the other day. I promised not to tell the truth until after he died. But from what he said about your brother, he wanted you to know."

Tye glanced over at Lexie's face. The only way to describe her expression was a mixture of shock and joy.

"This is probably not the time, but I'll say it anyway. I'm glad you're my nephew, Adam." Lexie reached her hand toward him. He held it for a second then walked out of the room.

"Wow! You know how to wake a girl. How long have you known about Adam?"

"Not very long. I hope he'll forgive us for messing with his life."

"I'm sure he will." Lexie smiled.

"Damn, you're happy for a woman whose brother is about to have an emotional crack-up."

"Not every day that I get a nephew. I like the thought of being Aunt Lexie."

"It may take him a long time to accept us," Tye warned.

"You maybe, but I'm really nice. He'll like me long before you 'cause I didn't do anything that requires forgiveness."

Tye laughed, "I think those pills are making you loopy."

"I tell the truth, brother dear, drugged or not."

"Jamie needs to be told, so that's my next mission. I hope she handles it better than our son. I'll take you home in the morning."

"Okay. Congratulations!"

Guilt dampened Tye's spirit as he drove toward Jamie's house. He knew Adam hurt, but he couldn't help picking up on Lexie's happiness over having Adam in their lives. To have a son was an impossible dream, and now he had two."

Jamie came to the door in a terry robe. "This is an unexpected visit."

"I wanted to tell you in person."

"What?"

"Dr. Carr told me that Adam Cox is our son."

"Oh, my God!" she cried out. Tye held her close.

"Does he know about us?" Jamie questioned.

"He does now. It'll take him a while, but I think he'll come around."

"Where are his adoptive parents?"

"They were killed in a plane crash. That's why Adam moved to Diffee—to live with his grandpa. Carr was in heart surgery tonight. Must have thought he was dying because he tried to tell Adam the truth."

"Shouldn't we be with our son?"

Tye shook his head. "He needs time. I'll drop back by the hospital to see how Carr is doing."

Jamie gave him a quick kiss on the cheek.

Tye wondered about the questions Jamie didn't ask. When the shock wore off, he'd get an earful for withholding information.

✦✦✦✦✦

The lady at the hospital information desk offered a friendly smile that Tye didn't return. "How is Dr. Carr doing?"

"Dr. Carr delivered my daughter thirty years ago. He's a good guy."

"I agree. How is he?"

"He's stable. The surgery went well. You just missed his grandson. Said he had to feed their animals."

"Thanks."

Tye returned to his apartment for a sleepless night.

Epilogue

Tye and Red ordered Lexie to stay home two days. They threatened all sorts of medieval tortures if she didn't comply. Today was her first day back at work. It was good to see the flowers on Delia's desk and the unmatched file cabinets.

Delia jumped from her chair at the sight of Lexie. "My dear girl, how are you doing?"

"The town heroine returned to work," Tye announced. "Quite the story Adam wrote about you in the paper."

"Adam has a flair for the overstatement."

Delia hugged her. "You deserved every word of it."

Lexie felt the comforting fit of her old chair. "Delia, will you get breakfast for the three of us at Dixie's?"

"Are pancakes and bacon okay?"

"Perfect."

Lexie turned to Tye after Delia left. "How's Beth?"

"She's got a long road to recovery, but they say she'll make it."

"Turner?"

"He died, Sis. Lost too much blood."

"I feel guilty about that. He was just helping us out, not even his job."

"I still find it hard to believe that Mariah murdered her friends." Tye acknowledged.

Lexie verbalized her belief. "For someone born a male, who wanted to be female, it was the ultimate prize—First Lady of the United States."

The room was quiet for a few moments.

Lexie traced the scar down the side of her face. "It's time

to find our father's killer."

"We will find him," Tye promised. "And my other son?" Her hand reached to grasp his.

"Yes," she answered. "We will find them both; one out of hatred, and the other out of love."

Acknowledgements

I would like to thank the following individuals, who provided encouragement, and recommendations during the writing process: Poet Rae Neal, Author Karen Cornell, Author Susan Case, Author Maureen McMahon, and Author Peggy Fielding. A special 'thank you' to former Pawnee County Sheriff Roger Price. Sheriff Price gave insights into the role and duties of an Oklahoma sheriff. Thank you to my daughters, Amy Grimes Price and Kimberly Grimes Roberts, who cheered me on, and are the joys of my life.

Cover Art: Tara Mayberry, www.teaberrycreative.com

More Sheriff Lexie Wolfe Novels

Deadly Search-Book 2

Sheriff Lexie Wolfe is entangled in a web of deceit as she searches for her father's murderer. Her mother may be the reason Lexie's father was killed. If she finds her father's killer, what price will she pay for revenge?

Terror's Grip-Book 3

Lexie's right arm suspends above her, held by a chain attached to a two-inch metal clamp around her wrist. The chain trails through a broken cellar window. Her left hand fists and punches forward as if a boxing bag, or her captor's new face, dangles in front of her. Lexie's scream fills the cold darkness.

"I WON'T DIE WEAK!"

Murder and Beyond-Book 4

Sheriff Lexie and Deputy Tye Wolfe are enmeshed in the strangest cases of their law enforcement careers. Two teenage girls vanish. Tye doesn't believe that Wendy is a witch. Lexie doesn't think the ocean swallowed Emma.

Deranged Justice-Book 5

Local citizens panic when Sheriff Lexie doesn't solve a series of bizarre murder cases. She is removed from office pending an investigation of incompetence and criminal activity. An irrationally jealous woman and a man who demands custody of Lexie's adopted nephew add more turmoil to her life.

Her Dying Message-Book 6

Sheriff Lexie's tears blur the body that lies face down on the rocks. Her scream catches in the wind and carries to the treetops. A family member was shot at close range—murdered. Her pursuit of evidence is hampered by a puzzling question. Why kill a good person for someone else's sins?

Visit the author's website: www.donnawelchjones.com

Made in the USA
Columbia, SC
23 June 2021